BETRAYED!

Humbolt had betrayed him. The plot to fake the murder and turn the Lorr on his trail reeked of his political manipulations.

"We have reached a unanimous decision," the agent-general said. "Normal crimes are punishable by local imprisonment. This is no ordinary crime." The Lorr shivered delicately.

"Barton Kinsolving, you are hereby sentenced to life imprisonment on the world with no name. Exile to this world is permanent. Starships land prisoners. No one ever leaves.

"Ever."

MASTERS OF SPACE

THE STELLAR DEATH PLAN

ROBERT E. VARDEMAN

AVON
PUBLISHERS OF BARD, CAMELOT, DISCUS AND FLARE BOOKS

MASTERS OF SPACE: THE STELLAR DEATH PLAN is an original publication of Avon Books. This work has never before appeared in book form. This work is a novel. Any similarity to actual persons or events is purely coincidental.

AVON BOOKS
A division of
The Hearst Corporation
1790 Broadway
New York, New York 10019

Copyright © 1987 by Robert E. Vardeman
Published by arrangement with the author
Library of Congress Catalog Card Number: 86-91012
ISBN: 0-380-75004-X

First Avon Printing: January 1987

AVON TRADEMARK REG. U.S. PAT. OFF. AND IN OTHER COUNTRIES, MARCA REGISTRADA, HECHO EN U.S.A.

Printed in the U.S.A.

K–R 10 9 8 7 6 5 4 3 2 1

For Mike Montgomery

THE STELLAR DEATH PLAN

CHAPTER ONE

THE BLARE of the siren brought Barton Kinsolving out of a deep sleep. He had partially dressed before he came fully awake and had reached the door to his small house before he even realized he responded to the undulating warning.

Thick, work-hardened fingers pressed shut the last fastener on his shirt as he dashed outside and into the compound. Already, harsh carbon-arc lights had come on all around.

"What's happened?" he yelled over the siren. A curly-haired woman shook her head. She appeared to be in a daze. Kinsolving cursed under his breath. This was the fourth time in as many weeks that the alarms had gone off. And each disaster deep within the bowels of the planet had been worse than the time before. Kinsolving hoped that this was only a short circuit, a false alarm, a mistake on a new recruit's part that would give him something to rail against, then peacefully return to his bed and sleep without nightmares.

His dark eyes focused on the rising plumes of bone-white smoke from the mouth of the distant mine shaft. The turbulent dust, sprinkled with flecks of mica that turned into artificial lightning bugs when the spotlight hit them, told the story. Kinsolving ran a hand through his hair and tried to calm himself. At this time of night it wasn't likely that many humans would be deep within the rare earth mines.

But what of the robot miners? Kinsolving cursed so loudly at the thought of losing another shift of the machines that several of his gathering co-workers edged away from him. He ignored them and ran to the control center.

"Ala!" he cried. He stopped just inside the door and looked at the lovely woman seated behind the console. Some of the anger at his sorry fate faded. When Ala Markken was near, things always went better for Kinsolving. He knew that wasn't strictly true, but it seemed that way and that was all that counted.

"Glad you got here, Bart," she said. Even mixed with the wail of the warning siren, her voice was level, low, sultry and exciting. "Stoop twenty-three went this time. Got a damp warning, then a gas release and..." She shrugged her shoulders. Kinsolving forced himself to concentrate on the readouts rather than the brief flash of bare shoulder she gave him.

He bent forward, frowning. A few minutes' work on the computer gave him numbers that weren't as bad as he'd expected—but were still far from pleasing.

"The robominer in the stoop failed to detect moisture and drilled through into an artesian spring. That's the only way it could have happened." He sighed. This shouldn't have happened. The robot sensory equipment was better than that—yet it *had* occurred.

"What about the gas indication?" the brunette asked him. "I got a strong positive reading for methane."

Kinsolving shook his head and straightened. "I think the sensors shorted out when the water hit them. We're going to have to drop a hose from number seventeen and pump out the water before we reopen."

"If we're lucky, you mean. There's no way to tell if the robot hit an underground river or just a trapped pocket of fossil water."

"There's a way. Send down the fiber optic probe. Check the rate of water flowing through the stoop, use visuals, use IR if necessary to find the robo-miner and see if we can't repair it by remotes, get it back online. You know the drill."

Ala turned and looked him squarely in the eye. "Bart," she said softly, "the foptic probe equipment is gone. It was on twenty. Water's already risen to nineteen." She tapped the readout on the control console for emphasis. "We're going to have to close three entire levels. Might even take more than that by the time we're finished."

"Level nineteen!" Kinsolving yelled. He spun and thrust aside an empty chair to get to another computer console. A cold lump formed in the pit of his stomach when he saw that the storage bins had been lost. The lanthanite and gadolinite holding areas were gone. The rare earth oxide ores were separated on level nineteen, then transported to the surface once a week when the heavy-lifter robots were brought over from the other mine shaft.

He had lost more than five days worth of output from the mine. Kinsolving reached over and pulled the chair toward him. He sank into it, the soft pneumatic wheezing of the chair adjusting to his burly frame equalling his own heavy sigh.

"I'm going to find myself in a dole line back on Earth for this one," he said. "Four years of good record, now this. Four major setbacks in as many weeks. I'm going to be fired and buried as deep as—as that robominer." Kinsolving pointed toward the steady red light glaring at him from the console indicating a malfunctioning miner unit.

"We're almost three months behind production quota," Ala told him. "The yields on the gandolinite and monazite haven't been up to assay."

The woman's fingers ran lightly over the panel until most of the red lights went out, replaced by blinking amber caution signals. This was all anyone could do until the mine was pumped and cleaned. She rose lithely and came to him, arms circling his neck. She held him close, her head resting next to his. Ala kissed his shoulder and turned her face slightly so that she looked around at him.

"It's not your fault," she said. "The powers that be at IM know that. You're a good engineer, Bart. A damned good one. They won't fire you over this. It's not your fault. The readouts will prove it."

"Mining is a dangerous profession," Kinsolving said, resting his hand on Ala's soft cheek. "But Humbolt made it clear that high production and no glitches were what he expected—or he'd replace me."

"Humbolt's a fool. What does he know about fieldwork? He sits at a desk all day and makes pointless decisions."

"He might be a fool," Kinsolving said, "but he's still our boss." Kinsolving swung around and let Ala sit on his lap. Her nearness usually pushed back the darkness he often felt, but this time his depression had plunged to too great a depth in his soul. Interstellar Materials held a ten-year lease to mine the rare earth oxides on this alien-held planet only through great diplomatic skill and immense fees paid on the precious 57–71 atomic number metals lifted from the surface. Barton Kinsolving had been drawn to IM because of the high salary—payable at the end of his contract—and the chance to leave Earth.

To leave Earth. He almost snorted in disgust. Earthmen had heaved themselves out to the stars a century earlier only to find a dozen alien races already populating the nearby star systems. Humans were less than an oddity—they were an annoyance to the older, better established races. Worst of all for a culture that had exhausted most of the resources of its planet, the juiciest plums had already been picked.

Deepdig was one such plum. The humanoid Lorr had established colonies on the planet fifty years before the first primitive starships had warped the four point three light years from Earth orbit to Alphacent. In the council of stargoing races, this century and a half of habitation gave the Lorr full rights to the planet's exploitation. Kinsolving had no idea what IM had promised the Lorr in exchange for the rare earth oxides, but he knew it had to be significant.

Earth needed the gadolinium and cerium for optical glasses and the lanthanum for fiber optics. Most of all it needed the pink and green samarium salts for use in the stardrives. Without it, the starspanning engines wouldn't function reliably. And without a dependable stardrive, Earth would again be isolated and choking in its own debris.

Kinsolving held Ala close, her warmth driving away some of the tenseness in his body and her scent making him feel things would work out.

"I've got to go down into the mine," he said at length. Reluctantly, he pushed her away.

"You take this too personally, Bart," she said. "Accidents happen."

He started to ask why she hadn't picked up the robot's sensor signal indicating water and turned off the unit, but he held back. Ala Markken was more than his lover, she was the best technician on his crew. Too many of the others had rotated through, going on to other jobs with Interstellar Materials.

Ala had stayed for the full four years he had been here.

Only her presence had saved his sanity. The Lorr inspectors were openly hostile, existing only to find minute violations of their intricate safety and lifting agreements. Humbolt came to Deepdig once a planetary year for on-site inspections. Ala placated him and acted as a buffer between corporate director and mine supervisor. For this alone, Kinsolving loved her.

He stared at her soft brunette hair, her deep, penetrating eyes, the face that rivalled any tri-dee star's. Ala Markken had been a minor functionary at IM's headquarters on Gamma Tertius 4 before coming to Deepdig. He had always wondered why she had left the heart of corporate power and had asked her once, getting no real answer. Ala could have progressed far up the IM corporate structure by now if she'd remained at headquarters. But she had chosen to do fieldwork.

Kinsolving was glad that she had. The four years at this mine would have been intolerable without her. And the past few months would have driven him to suicide.

Robot miner breakdowns, lower grade ore than expected, now this major disaster.

"All units are gone, Bart," she said. "Why not order over the heavy-lifters from the other mine and work back down? The ore bins on level nineteen might be intact."

He shook his head. Kinsolving knew better than to hope for a miracle of this scale. "If the robot dug into a river, the surge would have scattered the ore and put the separated dust into collodial suspension. Who knows where it has washed to by now?"

"No way to siphon off the water and distill it?"

He didn't laugh at her. Kinsolving knew that Ala's knowledge of computers was without limit but her instincts about mining operations left something to be desired.

"No way," he said.

"It's not your fault. Not even Humbolt can blame you for the shoddy equipment they send out. It's been malfunctioning for months and months. It's a wonder that you've been able to hold it together."

"I know," Kinsolving said. He frowned. When he had come to work on Deepdig only the finest robot equipment had been shipped to him. Why send broken-down units forty-nine light years from Gamma Tertius 4? Especially when the rare earths were so desperately needed by Earth? Kinsolving wondered if Humbolt—or someone at operations and supply on GT 4—wasn't siphoning off funds for the top of the line equipment and sending the cheapest robominers available.

"What now?" Ala asked.

"We follow the logged procedures. Call the Lorr representative, get him out to investigate. I'll send a message packet to Humbolt. He'll probably want to drag his fat ass out here to personally fire me."

"Bart," Ala chided gently.

"All right, all right, no more self-pity. Get on the com-line and arrange for the Lorr agent. I'll see if anything can be done down in the mine."

"Be careful," Ala said. She bent and gave him a quick kiss.

"For more of that, I'll be *damned* careful," he said, smiling a little.

Ala Markken turned back to begin the report that would summon the Lorr. Kinsolving left the control center and shouted orders to his human workers as he walked to the mouth of the mine shaft. Seldom did humans enter the underground world of the rare earth mine. At the periphery of the hole stood a wide variety of computerized equipment, all the inputs funneled to Ala Markken in the control center.

It didn't surprise Kinsolving to find that no humans had been on duty at the shaft. As long as no trouble developed, Ala was capable of running the entire operation.

"Who was scheduled to be on-site?" he asked. Kinsolving looked around the small circle of technicians. No one volunteered the information. "Garibaldi, check it out for me. Get the roster up and on a screen where I can see it."

The man tapped in the request. Kinsolving peered over his shoulder as the data emerged from the control computer. Kinsolving frowned and ran a hand through his sweat-lank hair at the answer.

"Keep checking," he said. "I don't believe no one was scheduled to be out here."

"No one was, Mr. Kinsolving," spoke up the curly-haired woman he had seen back in the compound. Nina Porchek pushed through the crowd. "I told Ala she'd missed posting anyone to oversee operations tonight but she said I didn't know what I was talking about. If someone had been present, the robominer might have been shut down in time when its automatic cutoff failed."

Kinsolving frowned even more. Nina Porchek was a replacement for a transfered computer operator. Her interests lay more with promotion to a management post than mine output. She had seen Kinsolving's attachment to Ala and had instantly resented the brunette. Kinsolving had little time for such politics.

But he saw that Porchek was right. If an operator had been present at the mine shaft controls, this would have given another chance to shut down before such extensive damage occurred.

"We've had too much equipment failure in the past few months," Kinsolving said. "I want a full maintenance check of all circuits, plus a visual of all mechanicals."

Groans of protest rose.

"Get to it now," Kinsolving said, voice cold. "Section chiefs, I want detailed reports by dawn. The Lorr representative will accept no less. I'm not going to be the one to lose IM's lease on Deepdig. Get to work. Now!" Kinsolving took no pleasure seeing the twenty hasten to their chores. He was left alone with his thoughts to stare down into the dark mouth of the shaft.

The rising dust had settled. Straining, Kinsolving heard the deep, dangerous rumble of water eighteen hundred meters below. Level twenty-three, another forty meters deeper, would be impassable except by sophisticated rescue equipment—which he didn't have.

Kinsolving made a cursory examination of the monitoring equipment, then started down into the mine. Nina Porchek called out to him, "Mr. Kinsolving! You're not supposed to go down alone! That's against the rules!"

"Give me your com-link. And get back to work."

"But the safety regs say—"

"Back to work," he snapped. He was in no mood to argue over such trivial matters with a power-hungry underling. Kinsolving took her com-link and switched it to central control frequency. He flipped the Attention toggle until Ala Markken answered.

"Ala, this is Bart. I'm going to look around a bit down in the mine shaft."

"No, wait, Bart, wait!"

"I'll be fine," he said, angry that she would duplicate Porchek's objection. "Kinsolving, out." He savagely thumbed off the unit. The flashing red indicator showed that Ala tried to reach him. He kept the sound off. Let it record and nothing more, he decided. The com-link's optical and audio sensors would pick up much that he missed with a visual inspection.

Swinging down the steps two at a time brought him to level one. Kinsolving took the time to put on a heavy respirator. In spite of his feeling that only water had invaded the lowest levels of the mine, Ala had gotten a transient indication of gas. The com-link would warn him of unsafe air, but Kinsolving preferred to avoid the chance of a microburst of methane rendering him unconscious for even a few seconds. Such might prove deadly in a mine inoperative due to disaster.

He found a hand flash and shone the brilliant light along the equipment shaft. Kinsolving saw nothing amiss; he descended to the next level. He wished that he dared use the elevator but as long as the water boiled at level nineteen, it was more prudent to leave off any electrical power to avoid further equipment damage.

He smiled ruefully. He worried about equipment damage more than electrocution. Being supervisor for four years had given him a skewed picture of safety, at least for himself. Better to risk himself than either other human personnel or the increasingly precious robot mining equipment.

Kinsolving found the emergency ladder at the side of the shaft. He turned the flash down into the depths of the stygian cavern and shuddered. The light failed to pick out the raging torrent of water far below—but he heard its hellish din. Only luck would keep him from losing another level to the rising underground river.

Carefully descending, Kinsolving checked the readouts at every level, both on the permanently mounted equipment and on his com-link. Temperature rose, atmosphere remained breathable although he kept his respirator on, the automated mining equipment worked independently and well. Kinsolving shook his head. It was always this way, it seemed. The levels with the lowest grade ores had the least problems. As he continued on his way down past the fifth level, Kinsolving felt a shivering in the ladder's plastic rungs.

The power came back on, the emergency lights momentarily blinding him. Ala had determined that no further damage would be done. Kinsolving heaved a sigh of relief as he swung into level six. His shoulders had begun to ache from the descent. He was glad he wouldn't have to climb back; his muscles would be sore for a week. For all the complaining he did about desk jockeys and petty bureaucrats, Kinsolving knew he was hardly better. What did he need muscle for when tireless robominers pulled out a kilogram of ore every minute of every twenty-hour day? The full automation of the rare earth mine allowed production unheard of, even back on Earth.

Kinsolving started to check in with Ala, then saw that the flashing light on the com-link still told of the woman's insistence to warn him back. Obstinately, Kinsolving ignored it and pressed the elevator call button. It came rumbling down from above; he swung in and found the control panel. Careful scrutiny showed danger warnings for every level below eighteen.

Kinsolving descended to seventeen.

As he stepped out, spray from ten meters below came up the shaft and soaked his clothing. He wiped clear the eye lenses of his respirator and peered down, shining the hand flash onto the churning surface of the water. The lowest levels of this mine might be closed permanently, he realized. For all his experience, he had never seen such complete destruction from water.

Kinsolving started to stand, then caught sight of

something that seemed out of place. His sharp cone of light came to rest on severed cables. Kinsolving pointed the com-link sensors at the cut while his mind raced. He knew the wiring diagrams for the mine by heart, but it took several seconds before he recognized this as a secondary control circuit. The robominer cut directly into the rock, following programmed instructions. This far underground, simple radio broadcast proved impossible and foptic or laser links too expensive or impractical. A hard wire came from the unit to a transmitter.

Kinsolving looked at the junction box for the robot miner's safety sensors.

Someone had cut the wire so that the robominer was unable to warn the operator when it encountered the underground river.

"Sabotage?" Kinsolving asked himself. His voice echoed strangely inside the respirator and he almost took it off. A quick, instinctive check of the com-link showed that the air was no longer breathable here. He needed the heavy mask to stay alive.

"It might have been cut by flying debris," he said. "That's it. Debris." Kinsolving wormed around on his belly, leaning far over the edge of the level eighteen elevator platform. The transmitter and the cut wire were still several meters lower; with the churning, frothy water in the shaft he wasn't sure what he saw.

Kinsolving pulled himself back onto the elevator platform when he found telltale gouges on the sides of the shaft that could have been made only by a heavy-lifter robot. An unauthorized use of such equipment constituted not only immediate dismissal by IM but also violated IM's agreement with the Lorr. They monitored every lifting of ore from the mine; their representative levied taxes on the spot. If a heavy-lifter had been used, that meant the Lorr had been cheated—and possibly that no ore had remained on level nineteen when the flooding occurred.

"Sabotage to cover the theft of rare earth ores," Kinsolving muttered. "But why?"

That proved impossible to answer. Interstellar Materials and the Lorr controlled all off-planet flight. How could anyone expect to sneak down, load such a massive quantity of ore—even reduced ore —and get away with it? And why? Any single lifting from the mine wouldn't be profitable enough for such piracy.

The words began to echo in Kinsolving's skull: Any single lifting.

What if the ore theft had been going on for some time? Months? Years? The value of such rare earths would be immense over a span of years.

That still didn't answer the question of who. And how. Starflight was too well controlled for a modern-day Captain Kidd aboard an interstellar pirate ship.

Kinsolving shook off such fanciful notions. He might never have noticed the heavy-lifter rock scars before. Coming down into the mine was an occasional trek for him. And the cut sensor circuit might have happened after the flooding. He began tinkering with control boxes powered by emergency fuel cells. Within ten minutes the powerful auxiliary pumps had begun their slow work. Another twenty minutes saw level eighteen pumped out, and Kinsolving watched as the churning water dropped lower and lower. He made a few quick estimates and decided that two more levels would be drained by morning.

He settled bone-tired onto the floor of the elevator and crossed his long legs. Wincing at the pain in his muscles, he reached up and pressed the ground level button.

The elevator shuddered and began the almost two kilometer climb to the surface.

It had gone only five hundred meters when the power failed. Aches forgotten, Kinsolving surged to his feet and slammed his fist hard against the emergency brake activator button.

He screamed inside his respirator when the braking failed. His stomach rose into his throat as the elevator plummeted back into the mine—back into the dark depths toward the flooded lower levels.

CHAPTER TWO

THE ROCKY, barren planet swung around a sun emitting far too much ultraviolet for comfortable human habitation, but humans did populate Gamma Tertius 4. From the stellar-radiation-cracked plains rose a magnificent spire that shone the purest jade green from multifaceted sides. Within this gleaming structure the board of directors for Interstellar Materials met.

At the head of the polished Earth-ebony table sat a small, wizened man hardly able to hold up his head. Every time Hamilton H. Fremont slumped tiredly to one side an attentive nurse gently shook his shoulder. The man motioned the nurse away with a weak gesture of a hand so pale and translucent that it might have been made of beige plastic. Only when seven others entered the room and took their places behind pneumatic chairs did the chairman of the corporation nod slightly. The nurse took a small packet from her uniform pocket and emptied the contents into a glass of water. The mixture sizzled and hissed and turned the distilled water a pale blue. She helped Fremont drink the stimulant. The seven waited with barely concealed impatience until the drug took control and transformed their chairman into a more dynamic person.

"Be seated," Fremont ordered in a voice surprisingly strong and deep for one in such debilitated condition. Shaky hands rested on the black wood table in front of him, Fremont leaned forward slightly. "There is a problem on Deepdig. Report, Mr. Humbolt."

Kenneth Humbolt cleared his throat and tried to hide his nervousness. Nothing escaped Fremont's sharp gaze. Not for the first time, Humbolt wished he knew the secret of the potion given Fremont by his nurse. If such a drug turned a doddering, senile old man into an executive capable of running a star-spanning financial empire, what would it do to a man a quarter as old and twice as ambitious?

"Mr. Chairman, members of the board," Humbolt began.

"You may skip the preamble. I am old and have no time left for such time-wasting maneuvers. Get on with your report. Deepdig. The rare earth mines. The troubles we are having there. You *do* remember, don't you, Humbolt?"

"Yes, sir," Humbolt said, damning the old man, while trying to retain his composure. He was a member of the board of one of the most powerful conglomerates in human-controlled space. He had earned the position. He had *earned* it! He wouldn't let Fremont intimidate him.

But the old man's presence did cause Humbolt real discomfort.

"The Lorr representative has expressed extreme displeasure with our operations in Deepdig number two," Humbolt said. He had no need to refer to his notes. The report burned brightly, deep in his mind. With responsibility for ten different mining operations on four planets, Humbolt could stay abreast of only the general matters, but Deepdig presented distinct problems of importance to more than just the IM profit margins.

"Will we be forced to negotiate once more?" asked Vladimir Metchnikoff from Humbolt's right.

"No. The Lorr consider us as only bungling inferiors. There is no hint that they know of the Plan or how the liftings from Deepdig number two enter into it."

"It'd be your head if they had even an inkling," snapped Fremont. "What of production? What of the flooding?"

"Mine supervisor Kinsolving had regained control of the situation much quicker than anticipated and had begun pumping three flooded levels, leaving only the lowest three closed. The rare earths storage area has been cleared."

"He knows?" asked Metchnikoff.

"There is no way he couldn't have discovered the sabotage and pilfering of the oxides," Humbolt said, angry that Metchnikoff forced such a confession. Humbolt felt his power slipping and Metchnikoff's star rising. The flux of influence on the board was always thus. Humbolt would have to salvage what he could and continue, perhaps undermining Metchnikoff's transport division in some fashion.

His brief inattention brought a stern reprimand from Fremont.

"Sorry, sir," Humbolt said, feeling like a small child caught stealing his parent's credit access. "Kinsolving is too efficient in his cleanup procedures. My office had estimated at least six months' work to pump down to the storage area, by which time we would have been able to justify total loss of the ores."

"The Lorr have put in an inquiry?"

"No, sir. Not yet, but I am sure that they will. We were lifting six thousand kilos of high-grade ore a week, of which fully half was not being counted and taxed by the Lorr agent. The intentional flooding of the mine would have hidden another twenty thousand kilograms of output from the Lorr."

"But not now," prodded Fremont.

"No, sir, not now." The words burned like acid on

Humbolt's tongue. "We have done what we can to correct this."

"Is this Kinsolving so efficient that he should be promoted?" asked Fremont. The old man's eyes fixed dagger-hard on Humbolt.

"It was necessary to sacrifice him in another 'accident,'" said Humbolt.

"Another accident?" Fremont coughed. His nurse handed him a small handkerchief to wipe his lips. "Unfortunate. This Kinsolving seems the sort we need to carry out the Plan."

"His profile did not indicate that, sir," said Humbolt. "He was stubborn and—"

"A quality we need. What did he feel about the damned Bizarres running the universe and holding us back?"

"There's some evidence to show that Kinsolving felt that the Bizzies, such as the Lorr, were acting within acceptable limits," Humbolt said carefully.

"You mean he was a goddamn traitor, that he sympathized with aliens over his own kind?" Fremont's anger caused a flush to come to his pale, wrinkled face.

"Yes, sir, that seems true."

"He's better off dead. How did you arrange it? Never mind. That's merely a detail."

"Our agent is very efficient, sir. I recommend promotion to headquarters."

"Promotion first to mine supervisor. We need those rare earths, dammit. We can't build the Bizzie brain-burners without them. And new starships can't be built without samarium. You know that, Humbolt. After we've milked what we can out of the Bizarres on Deepdig, then you will promote. Understood, Mr. Humbolt?"

"As you wish, sir."

Humbolt sat down, his legs shaking in reaction. Nothing had gone right with his scheme to increase the lift from the Deepdig oxide mines. The carefully orchestrated accident had attracted Lorr attention. If they checked the records with their usual dedication, they would find exactly how many kilos of the precious rare earths had been stolen. With this information shared with other Bizzie species, they might stumble onto a small portion of the Plan.

Humbolt shuddered, then tried to cover the involuntary reaction by rearranging the papers in front of him. His life would be forfeit if Fremont thought any part of the Plan had been revealed, even one as insignificant as the five-times-larger-than-declared Earth starship fleet. The Bizzies allowed only so much commerce with their worlds; they controlled too much. Humbolt's anger began to mount against the unfairness of the alien strictures.

One day that would change. And he would live to see it. He would live to preside over it. He would enjoy distributing the brain-burners, too. That was small enough retribution for the Bizarres holding back the human race!

Humbolt jerked around and came out of his reverie to hear Vladimir Metchnikoff complete a favorable report on IM's fleet growth, both declared and clandestine. The woman to Metchnikoff's right stood. Humbolt watched her with some lust and a great deal of fear. Maria Villalobos had risen quickly in IM ranks and was the youngest at the table. Humbolt wasn't sure that she wasn't also the most diabolical—and, from corporate spy reports on her personal habits, the most depraved.

Metchnikoff was an annoyance to Humbolt. Villalobos would be a major stumbling block unless he found a way of using her against Fremont, cancelling the influence and power of both the chairman of IM and an able opponent.

"Mr. Chairman," the small, dark, intense woman began. "As Director of Security I have identified

several problems within the corporate headquarters. Two employees have been...terminated."
The feral gleam in her eyes told Humbolt that the
pretty woman enjoyed this "termination." He wondered where the bodies had been hidden, if Villalobos left behind such crass evidence of her
handiwork.

"Were they Bizzie agents?"

"The Plan and our part in it has not been compro-
mised," Villalobos assured Fremont. "I have taken
steps to tighten security procedures and have hired
an enforcement officer of unparalleled reputation to
expedite matters off-planet."

"Who is this?" asked Metchnikoff.

"I am sure you have heard of Cameron," Villalobos said with obvious gusto.

Vladimir Metchnikoff paled. Humbolt looked
around the table at the other directors. None spoke
up to protest the hiring of such a bloody-handed assassin.

"Cameron?" asked Fremont. "The one who did the
work for us last year on Loki 2?"

"Yes, sir. The man is a noted expert on robotic
tracking and has a reputation for tenacity and...
remorselessness."

"That's one word for it," Humbolt said. Villalobos'
dark eyes flared like rocket blasts in the night. He
quickly said, "I put a motion before the board to not
only approve of Cameron's hiring but also to com-
mend Director Villalobos for such a brilliant use of
personnel."

This quieted Villalobos and forced the others on
the board to approve Cameron. To openly challenge
Villalobos now, they would also have to take on
Humbolt. While he might not be in as high standing with Chairman Fremont as before the Deepdig
debacle, Humbolt still wielded considerable influence at Interstellar Materials.

Humbolt smiled slightly and nodded in Villalobos' direction. The woman and he were not considered allies by the others—especially Metchnikoff, from the cold stare he received from the man. Humbolt smiled a little more. Was that betrayal flickering across Metchnikoff's face? Were the rumors about him and Villalobos being lovers true? What would Villalobos' passion be like? Humbolt would have to delve further into that to see if a more powerful wedge might be driven between the pair.

"Finance. Give me a finance report, Mr. Liu."

Humbolt leaned back and half listened to the march of numbers given by IM's financial genius. The corporation was in sound condition but if any alien auditor demanded their books as a condition of trade on a Bizarre-held world, the Bizzies would find only a tottering giant made of paper and hot air and borrowed funds.

One day that would change. Humbolt and the others worked for it. Interstellar Materials' part in the Plan might be small compared to others', but all humans and their talents would be needed. Even ones like Villalobos and her pet killer, Cameron.

CHAPTER THREE

THE IMPACT of the elevator platform against the surface of the water knocked Barton Kinsolving flat. He fell heavily and rolled to one corner of the elevator. Dirty water sloshed up. Dazed, he struggled to sit up. The world spun in crazy circles around him; a large knot at the back of his head oozed sticky blood. Just touching the spot sent laser cuts of pain into his head.

Kinsolving tried to stand. He fell back, too weak to accomplish even this simple task. Hip deep in water he sat, trying to regain his senses. Slowly, everything fit into a broader pattern. The power to the elevator had failed; he had plunged downward. The emergency brakes had caught but had scant time to slow the descent. Hesitantly, Kinsolving reached out to touch the brake assembly. He jerked back when the blistering hot metal burned his fingertips.

Cursing, he fought to his feet. The level of water rose to his thighs now. The elevator platform sank inexorably into the murky, watery bowels of the mine. Kinsolving tried to set the brakes more securely and failed. He used his hand flash to examine the area around. He had fallen just past level nineteen.

Struggling to open the elevator's restraining door, he found some slight support to climb up to nineteen. Panting, he lay on the rocky floor until he re-gained his strength.

Kinsolving shook himself as dry as he could, then got to his feet. The sharp light from the flash showed the extensive damage done by the flood waters, but even more revealing were the empty storage bins. The waters hadn't rushed past long enough to erase the mark left by the recent passage of a heavy-lifter. All the rare earth oxides had been taken before the flooding.

Of this Kinsolving had no doubt.

He rummaged around in the level nineteen storage area but found no clue to the thief—and sabo-teur.

Kinsolving checked his com-link and found it still functional. He moved its sensor around to record what he could, but he had no illusions about finding the thief—or thieves. Finishing, he slung the de-vice at his hip and returned to the elevator shaft. The platform had continued to sink and was now half-submerged. The pumps worked noisily to re-move the water from the lower stoops, but the ele-vator was lost to him.

Even if he had been able to restart the elevator, Kinsolving didn't like the notion of rising a dozen levels only to have it repeat the power loss. A sec-ond time would completely destroy the brakes— and undoubtedly kill him.

Kinsolving looked up into the darkness. A tiny spot of light showed at the mouth of the shaft. Kin-solving wondered if this meant sunrise or the carbon-arc spotlight. He hadn't worn his watch and had the feeling of considerable time passing. Sigh-ing, he reached down to his belt and pulled free the com-link and plugged it into the respirator's cir-cuitry. He toggled the call button.

"Are you there, Ala? Come in, Ala. I'm trapped on level nineteen. Elevator's not operational." Even as the words came from his lips, fat blue sparks jumped up from below as the final elevator circuits shorted out.

"Ala, come in. I don't want to climb almost two kilometers to the surface. Can you send help? Over."

The com-link's indicator lights shone but otherwise gave no evidence of the device working. Kinsolving toggled the button a few more times and got a soft hiss indicating that the unit still functioned. But he got no response from above.

Cursing, he slung the com-link once more at his belt and reached up to grab the plastic rungs of the escape ladder leading to the surface. His shoulders protested the strain and by the time he had gone up four levels Kinsolving felt faint and nauseated. He rested on level fourteen and once more tried to raise Ala Markken.

When he failed, he again began to climb. This time Kinsolving got two levels before tiring. He curled up in the middle of the stoop and, shivering and cold and aching, dropped off into a heavy sleep that was more a coma.

The rumble of equipment coming down the shaft woke Kinsolving. The rush of hot air past his face and the concussion from an explosion far below him knocked him back a dozen paces. He sat down heavily and simply stared, dazed and unable to move.

The gases and heavy dust filled level twelve and obliterated what vision he had through his respirator lenses. Kinsolving worked on them a few minutes and succeeded in activating the infrared sensor in the left eyepiece. One-eyed, he moved through the dense fog until he came to the shaft. Shining his hand flash downward availed him nothing, but the IR eyepiece gave a chilling picture of destruction — and what would have been his death if he'd remained on any of the lower levels.

The heavy-lifter had fallen from level one and crashed into the top of the elevator cage, totally destroying its locked brakes and plunging it to the lowest level—under water. The collision between the falling heavy-lifter and the stalled, disabled elevator had produced a minor explosion and enough heat to dispel the bone-chilling cold, even seven hundred meters up-shaft.

Kinsolving sucked in a deep breath, took off the respirator long enough to wipe away the sweat damming up against his bushy eyebrows, then put the heavy mask back on. The stale air coming through the filter bothered his sinuses and made his nose clog and begin dripping, but he knew it was better than not breathing at all. One glance at the air quality indicator mounted at the edge of the shaft told him how deadly Deepdig number two had become.

Looking up the shaft, Kinsolving saw a steady bright light. Definitely daylight, he decided. Once more he pulled out the com-link and, holding it out into the shaft to prevent signal damping by the heavy rock, he called, "Ala, come in, Ala. This is Bart. Are you there? Is anyone there?"

The mocking hiss gave no indication that any human lived above. Kinsolving wondered if there'd be any alive in the shaft much longer. His arms and legs had turned to lead and the brief rest hadn't given him back lost strength.

"Up we go," he said. As he climbed, he worried over the theft of the rare earths, Ala Markken, their last vacation together on the seacoast, the number of days left until his contract was completed, anything to keep from thinking about the pain gathering in joints and muscles.

Level ten came and went. Barton Kinsolving rested. And once more he tried the com-link.

No good, he finally decided. The receive mode

might work—the hiss told him that much. But somewhere in his travails he had damaged the transmitter circuit. His luck had been like that lately. The one item to fail was always the vital one.

Two more levels. Rest. Weakness flooded him just as the water did the mine tunnels below. Darkness. The sun setting? Or had he fallen into unconsciousness? Kinsolving couldn't decide.

More climbing. One level. Rest. Two. Two more. Voices echoing from above. The sound of heavy-duty cycle pumps laboring to remove water from the flooded levels.

Kinsolving had no idea what level he had reached. Four? Two? He swung in from the shaft and the interminable plastic rungs and fell to the floor at the feet of a dozen technicians.

He didn't even remember them carrying him back to his quarters.

Sunlight fell across his face, warm and soothing. Kinsolving moaned slightly as he rolled over in bed, this small motion enough to activate every pain center in his body.

"Don't move, Bart," came Ala's worried voice. "The doctor did the best he could, but he said there really wasn't much wrong with you. Just exhaustion. He gave you a light sedative."

"Not much wrong?" Kinsolving fought to sit up. Weakness surged and threatened to rob him of bodily control. He pushed it back, refusing to give in. "He ought to be inside my skin. Bet a kilo of cerium he wouldn't say that then."

"What happened?" the woman asked. She sat on the edge of his bed and took his plasti-skin bandaged hand in hers. "You went down in the shaft, then we lost contact."

"I took along a com-link. Thought that would let me stay in touch. I must have hit it. Transmitter went out."

"Nina found it hooked onto your belt. It was her unit."

"Have you done a dump on its memory? I want a full—"

"Calm down, Bart." The expression on Ala's lovely face made Kinsolving wary.

"What happened to the unit?"

"I checked it out. The circuitry was entirely destroyed. Nothing recorded from the minute you took it from Nina."

"Nothing?"

Ala looked away, then her dark eyes came back and fixed squarely on his. "Nothing," she said.

"There's more. What's happened?"

"You . . . the heavy-lifter. It fell down the shaft. I don't know how it happened. Weak stanchion, I just don't know."

"It missed me. I was resting just inside the shaft on level twelve."

Ala nodded slowly. Kinsolving didn't like that look on her face at all.

"Who ordered it into the mine? It wasn't due for another three days."

"I'm sorry, Bart," she said. "I'm responsible. I thought we might lower the heavy-lifter and salvage some equipment."

"What caused it to fall?"

"We're checking into that. A new recruit might have missed a few of the security dogs. Or maybe the bolts weren't fastened tightly enough. We don't know yet. But we will. I promise!"

"What more's gone wrong at the bottom?" Kinsolving asked, changing the subject. "I started the auxiliary pumps and had two levels drained. I remember hearing the primary pumps before I passed out."

"The levels are flooded again, Bart. All the way up to fifteen. I've put in a request to headquarters for complete rescue equipment. We're lucky it wasn't worse."

Kinsolving said nothing. When he had started the auxiliaries, the water had gone down swiftly. With all pumps functioning, level twenty-three should have been dry once more.

"Who was in charge? While I was below?"

The question took Ala by surprise. "I was," she said. "I didn't know you'd gone down, though. You should have told me. Taken a command com-link instead of Nina's. Something!"

Kinsolving sensed a mixture of emotions fighting inside the woman. He reached out a bandaged hand and lightly brushed her cheek. A tear had formed and had begun a slow track down.

"Don't cry," he said. He bent forward gingerly and kissed her.

"I'll be in central control. You rest, Bart. The Lorr agent-general will be out tomorrow to investigate. You'll have to deal with him. You know how they are about humans."

Kinsolving knew. The Lorr dealt only with those in charge and refused to acknowledge the presence of any human underling. He had never decided if they ran their own society in this way or if it merely showed contempt for those they considered inferiors. Kinsolving didn't like the Lorr agent-general personally but he had some sympathy for their position. Allowing another race to exploit valuable resources might seem ridiculous, but Kinsolving had found that the Lorr lacked the mining equipment and technology, and pride kept them from buying it from humans.

Kinsolving settled back on the bed, sunlight warming his aching body. He closed his eyes and listened intently. For a long minute, Ala Markken stayed beside his bed. Then she left quickly. The click of the door sliding shut told him she had gone.

Kinsolving opened his eyes cautiously and looked around the room. All seemed intact, nothing disturbed, nothing added.

The uneasiness mounted within him, however. Something *was* amiss. It took careful study to find the answer. His desk com-link had been turned around so that it faced a blank wall. His first thought was that Ala had stood beside the desk to use it, but that wasn't physically possible. She would have had to bend over the top of the com-link. Better to turn it around or leave it where it had been.

Hating himself for being so paranoid, Kinsolving carefully rose from the bed, moving slowly and making no sound. On bare feet he went to his desk and studied the side of the com-link facing his bed. The small scratches on the side plate showed how it had been tampered with.

What had been placed inside? Kinsolving guessed that it was a sensitive audio pickup since the opaque casing of the com-link didn't provide for visual spectrum optics. He looked closer to be sure no foptic cable poked out; it didn't. This wasn't a good job of spying, done hurriedly and with whatever material was at hand.

Who had done it?

Kinsolving didn't want to face the answer to that question.

Moving carefully, he pulled on clothing and slipped into the sanitary chamber. Kinsolving finished dressing, wincing at the leftover agony arrowing into his body from the ordeal in the mine. Climbing through the small window and dropping to the ground outside, he made his way to the records computer behind central control.

As he silently passed the opened door of the control room he saw Ala Markken hunched over the com-panel. He couldn't hear her words but judging from her expression she was speaking with someone she'd rather avoid.

Kinsolving entered the empty records room and went directly to the storage computer. He settled in a chair and tried to make himself comfortable.

"Couldn't afford a pneumatic chair," he grumbled, regretting the earlier economy on his part. Kinsolving reached out and called up production records, set up correlations, comparisons, ran charts, did a complete workup of mine output.

Two intense hours later, he sat back in the chair. His body still hurt, but a deeper agony now possessed him. The theft of the high grade rare earth oxides from the mine had been more extensive than he'd thought. The lifting masses failed to match the reduced ore masses by a factor of two. Fully half of everything mined at Deepdig number two had been stolen.

Seeing the evidence of the heavy-lifter and the empty ore storage bins on level nineteen had alerted him to this possibility. What hurt the most was his analysis of the person most likely to have done it.

He had suspected any of a half dozen people. All had opportunity, even if he couldn't understand what they would do with such massive amounts of stolen ore.

Any of six could have been responsible, and might be implicated. But Kinsolving had pinpointed the one person definitely a thief.

Ala Markken.

Barton Kinsolving felt sick to his stomach as he stood and went to confront her with the evidence.

CHAPTER FOUR

BARTON KINSOLVING'S LEGS wobbled under him as he made his way into the control center. Ala Markken hunched over the computer console and worked feverishly, then vented a deep sigh and leaned back. The light from the terminal caught her face and turned it soft, giving a vulnerability that Kinsolving now wondered about. He loved her, but his work seemed without mistake.

She had stolen a considerable amount of rare earth ore from Interstellar Materials—and had tried to kill him, not once but twice. Kinsolving stared at her, the light brown halo of hair floating about her and turning her into something more than mortal.

Ala stiffened slightly, sensing his presence. She turned and saw him standing beside the doorway.

"Bart, you shouldn't be up yet. You're not well."

"You thought the drugs would keep me out for another week, didn't you?" His tone carried a steel edge that made Ala stiffen even more.

"What are you saying? Of course the drugs would put you to sleep. You need it after all you've been through."

"After all you've put me through."

Her eyes narrowed. To her credit Ala Markken didn't try to argue, to profess ignorance. She turned back to the computer console and tapped in an access code. The parade of data told her the complete story of Kinsolving's probing.

"You'd never understand, Bart," she said softly. "I argued with them at first, but they won me over. I thought you might come around to our way of thinking, but it's not in you. I see that now."

"Why, Ala? You're well paid. Back on Earth eighty percent of everyone is jobless, on some form of dole. Most are merely existing."

"Subsistence living, they call it," Ala said bitterly. "We deserve more."

"You *have* more!" Kinsolving cried. He sank down to a chair. His legs had turned rubbery and he didn't know if he could continue much longer.

"Me? Oh, yes, I have more than most of those on Earth. I have a job and a good one."

"Why did you steal the ore, then?" Kinsolving blinked at her expression.

Ala covered it quickly. She said, "There's always need for more money. The rare earths are better than any currency. I can retire in another few months."

"You could have retired after stealing one storage bin of ore," he said. "A hundred kilograms of ore would reduce to enough to keep us all in luxury for the rest of our lives. It's more, Ala, it's got to be more. Why?"

"How much do you think I've stolen?"

"You've been doing it for years. I couldn't tell for sure but it looked as if you had started immediately after arriving. Four years of theft." Kinsolving shook his head. His tongue felt fuzzy and thick. His head pounded like the ground under a rocket exhaust and the aches in his body returned to slowly drain him of stamina.

"I have expensive tastes. You know that, Bart."

He sat, trying to keep from fainting. The only thing that allowed Kinsolving to keep some semblance of rationality was his driving need to find a way out for Ala. Condoning theft from IM wasn't really possible, he knew, and she would have to confess to the crime, but there had to be mitigating circumstances, some way to keep her from prison — or worse.

Kinsolving had heard that off-planet justice often entailed the death penalty. He tried to remember the covenants of business that IM worked under on Deepdig. Were such crimes the responsibility of the company or the Lorr?

"The Lorr," he said, all strength draining from his body. He slumped forward. "I'd forgotten about them. Stealing the ore means IM hasn't been paying severance taxes due the Lorr."

"They have strict penalties, Bart," Ala Markken said softly. "They might execute me."

"No, no, that won't happen. We... we'll tell Humbolt."

"He'll see that I'm punished," she said, almost seeming to enjoy taunting him.

"You'll have to stand trial somewhere. I'd prefer it in IM court with Earth laws rather than letting the Lorr try you."

"The Bizarres," she mused. "They seem to be the problem, don't they? Who was hurt? Not IM. Only the Bizzies aren't getting their blood money. Is that so bad, Bart?"

"Yes," he said with returning fire. "IM signed an agreement with them. We have to honor it."

"They're only aliens. And they only want to hold Earth back, keep us in grinding poverty. If it hadn't been for them, we'd be masters of the stars now, not second-raters begging for crumbs."

"That's not true and you know it. We caused our own problems on Earth, and we can work through them."

"If the Bizzies would let us."

"They couldn't care less about us. We're almost beneath their contempt."

"Exactly!"

"Ala, please. You broke the law and you must pay for it." Kinsolving wiped cold sweat from his forehead and closed his eyes for a second to try to still the violent hammering in his temples. The ache had turned to pain.

"You love me. I love you, Bart. Let's see if we can't hide this. What does it matter to the Lorr? I'll see that you get a cut. You'll be rich!"

Anger flooded Kinsolving and burned away aches, pain and weakness. "If you think that's all I want, you're wrong, Ala. Completely wrong."

"What have you done?" she asked suspiciously, seeing his new resolve.

"I've alerted Humbolt. Sent a message packet to GT 4."

"No." The single word barely came from her mouth.

"I don't like him, but—"

"You fool! The Lorr intercept every message packet and read the contents."

"I coded it."

"They know all our codes. All of them!"

Ala Markken fell back heavily in the chair and just stared at Kinsolving. He tried to read the emotion of that look and failed. It wasn't love or hate; it was inscrutable and all the more disquieting for that.

The Lorr investigators arrived at the mine less than an hour later.

"Is this a formal hearing?" asked Kenneth Humbolt. "If so, I feel that Interstellar Materials should be given the courtesy of adequate legal counsel."

The Lorr agent peered at Humbolt, face unreadable. Barton Kinsolving had tried for four years to find some trace of emotion in the aliens and had always failed. Their gray faces appeared to be chiseled from some strange, living granite, and he had never seen one that did not have squinting amber, pupilless eyes. The agent-general for Deepdig sat quietly behind a huge, cut stone table, fingers folding and unfolding in front of him in boneless ways not shared by humans. Other than this—a nervous gesture?—Kinsolving got no hint of the seriousness of the matter. He'd have to let Humbolt handle it, even though Humbolt had been less than responsive in the past six days since arriving.

Kinsolving frowned as he considered this. He'd sent the message packet directly to company headquarters on GT 4, almost fifty light years distant. Even with the supershift acceleration used by the message encapsulation, it couldn't have been received in less than three days. Humbolt had to have been en route and could never have read the contents of the packet, even though he claimed to have come in response.

Kinsolving wondered if Humbolt lied to keep an innocent facade in front of the Lorr. He had noticed Ala's attitude toward the aliens hardening more than it had been; if her feeling toward the Lorr was hard, Humbolt's was vicious and paranoid.

"This is a formal hearing to determine guilt," said the Lorr agent-general. The long fingers rippled, as if they were reflections in a pond rather than real digits. When the Lorr spoke, his thin lips pulled back in an expression similar to a human grimace, but no human's dark, pebbly tongue thrust from between lips to produce such a startling effect. And no human's teeth shone in a solid white dental plate. "There will be penalties assessed as a result of the findings this day."

"We demand counsel," said Humbolt in a voice too

loud for the small room. The gathered Lorr trained their pupilless eyes on him and remained silent.

"Mr. Humbolt," Kinsolving said softly. "Can we get the hearing postponed?"

"I tried," Humbolt said. "The Bizzies wouldn't do it. They want to convict us all right now."

"They were thorough going over the mine's shipment records," Kinsolving said. "It might be wise to admit guilt and take whatever punishment they have."

"Are you crazy?" Humbolt's eyes widened in shock.

"They're not stupid, Mr. Humbolt. We don't want to lose the rare earth mines for IM, do we? The Lorr might revoke our mining permit unless we do confess guilt." Kinsolving looked over at Ala Markken, who sat straight in a chair, eyes focused on a blank wall. Kinsolving had tried several times to talk to her and she had refused.

"The Bizzies won't go that far," Humbolt said, but no confidence rang in his voice on this point.

"What did she do with all the ore?" mused Kinsolving.

"What? Markken, you mean? Don't let it trouble you, Kinsolving. You're doing a fine job."

"I missed the pilfering. As mine supervisor, it was my duty to check everything, and I missed it." Kinsolving could barely bring himself to call the loss of over one hundred thousand kilograms of rare earth oxides "pilfering." He wasn't sure he had a word encompassing such a scale of theft, though.

"Primary among the charges against your company," spoke up the agent-general, "is fraud in not paying severance taxes." The Lorr twisted forward at an angle showing too few bones in his ribcage as he read the amounts. Kinsolving recoiled as a disagreeable odor rose. The Lorr's expression never changed but Kinsolving felt the extreme tension—

the alien's stench seemed to be an indication of loathing or fear of the humans. "Your supervisor and my auditors have agreed that taxes are delinquent on two hundred thousand kilos."

Humbolt held Kinsolving down at the inflated number. "Interstellar Materials agrees to pay these sums," Humbolt said, face pinched. "But we request graduated payments. The recent disaster at the mine has left us in precarious financial condition."

"No."

"But—"

"No," said the Lorr, voice flat and brooking no argument. "Further, we will in the future monitor onsite all liftings from the mine. No more can we allow your numbers to stand."

"This isn't part of our agreement," protested Humbolt.

"The amount of ore reaching your cargo ships is now in question," said the agent-general. He raised the curiously boned hand and the fingers rippled like tentacles. "We are investigating all avenues of exit from this planet to discover how the stolen ores were removed."

Kinsolving found himself nodding. This had bothered him, too. It appeared that Ala was guilty—and the other five he had suspected. But how had she removed the ore from Deepdig? That required the use of heavy equipment to move, to load, to get into orbit and onto a starship. And where did the stolen ore go? The amounts of pure samarium and the other rare earths might reach the tens of kilos by this time. Who could use such quantities without accounting for its source? Kinsolving knew that Earth authorities were meticulous in checking for contraband brought onto their home planet.

Still, a few kilos over four years could be missed by even the most careful of searches.

That did not answer the questions of who and

what did they do with material of such specific technological use.

"No fewer than five agent-captains will be stationed at each of your mines," the Lorr went on. "Their job will be to detect illicit activity detrimental to Lorr security and revenues. Any argument with them will constitute grounds for permanent revocation of Interstellar Materials' license."

"I protest. On the behalf of IM, I demand a hearing with legal counsel." Humbolt looked as if he'd been trapped and fought desperately to escape.

"Refused," the Lorr said. Kinsolving detected the first trace of emotion on the alien's part: triumph.

"We can live with it," Kinsolving said to Humbolt. The man spun and glared at him.

"We *can't* live with it, dammit," flared Humbolt.

"We retain the mining agreement," Kinsolving pointed out. Humbolt's expression told him that he was missing a key element in this. The ore was important to IM, but there was more. What? Kinsolving felt as if he'd been cast adrift and had lost sight of all land. And no one in the lifeboat would tell him where to paddle.

"How do we appeal this ruling?" called out Humbolt.

The Lorr bobbed his narrow head, amber eyes fixed on Humbolt. "This is the court of final rulings. You have lost in all lesser courts. My decision is final."

"But this is only the preliminary hearing!" Kinsolving blurted.

"You don't understand," said Humbolt. "They don't want us to win. They can make up whatever rules they want as they go along. This one puts their guards in the mines. Dammit!"

"This matter is closed," said the Lorr agent-general. "The next case is of lesser importance and has been decided." The Lorr pointed and Ala

Markken and the other five Kinsolving had decided were implicated in the ore theft were seized by the guards. "Take these to our prison to begin their sentences."

"Wait, you can't do this, you damned Bizzie!" shouted Humbolt.

The Lorr faced Kinsolving and said, "The agent-general and the Grand Council of Lorr thank Barton Kinsolving for his service in bringing these felons to justice."

"But I didn't do anything!" Kinsolving protested. He turned to Ala. Her eyes had widened in shock. Now fury burned in them—and it was directed at him.

"I didn't tell them anything. Ala, believe me. I didn't!"

The woman wasn't allowed to speak. The Lorr guards hurried her and the others from the room.

"Mr. Humbolt, I swear it. I never gave any evidence to the agent-general. He's lying!"

"His evidence came from somewhere," said Humbolt. The man heaved a sigh and sagged back in his chair. "I'm sorry, Kinsolving. I know you wouldn't betray any of your kind to a Bizarre."

"I don't have your...distaste for the Lorr," Kinsolving said, "but they're not my friends, either. I'd never willingly turn Ala over to them."

"You believe all that space gas put out about the Bizzies? Did you swallow it all without question?"

"What are you talking about?"

"Back on Earth. The appeasement faction in power now."

"I don't understand," said Kinsolving.

"They spew out all that shit about how we can live with the Bizzies, how they'll accept us if we're sweet and smile at our betters. They want to exist under the Bizzies' heel as slaves rather than as free men. That's the only way they think they can stay in power."

Humbolt's words came like a lecture—or a sermon. Kinsolving said, "I've got nothing against aliens. These—the agent-general—seems to carry a grudge against us. It might be directed at IM instead of at Ala and the others. He just sees a way to get even."

"We must keep them away from the mines," said Humbolt. He closed his case and stood. "Return to Deepdig number two and see if you can't get those lower levels opened. And if you happen to accidentally lose a few of the Bizzies, fine."

With that Kenneth Humbolt left the room.

Kinsolving watched and found himself beginning to despair. Ala Markken had been taken to prison, the impression given that he had been responsible. And Humbolt's attitude struck Kinsolving as totally wrong. Payment of the fine had galled the man, but having Lorr agents present at the mine site sent him into a real panic.

Why? Kinsolving felt that a world once logical and sane had turned upside down around him.

Worst of all, he wondered what new and terrible fate lay in store for him. He felt it coming, inexorably, and had no way of dodging.

CHAPTER FIVE

KENNETH HUMBOLT settled down in a chair and tried to relax. The man kept worrying over the problems posed by the Lorr agent-general—and the limitless trouble this would create with the board of directors. Humbolt had seen the chairman of the board angry before. Fremont usually downed his strength potion and rose, gnarled knuckles on the table, and then bellowed.

He bellowed and ranted and spat and the one on the receiving end of the tirade would try to sink into the floor. No one was strong enough, emotionally or politically, to endure the chairman's full wrath for longer than a few seconds.

Humbolt doubted such dismissal on Fremont's part was all that occurred. Not once had Humbolt ever heard of anyone after they had been removed from the board of Interstellar Materials. They vanished completely. Never did they appear on another company's board nor did they assume lesser roles in IM.

They disappeared without trace.

Humbolt rubbed his forehead nervously, hand coming away with sweat in spite of the air-conditioning working valiantly to keep the room at GT 4's lower mean temperature.

He finally realized that it wasn't the air conditioner that was failing. And this made Humbolt even more nervous. He leaned back in his chair and folded his arms tightly around himself, eyes closed to help him concentrate.

Things had glitched beyond his control. The flooding of the mine had gone according to schedule. It should have been enough to keep the Lorr agent-general and his auditors from ever determining the true output from the mine. No matter what the Lorr claimed, IM could make the counter that even more rare earth ore had been lost.

"Damn Kinsolving," he said aloud. He had appointed the man in spite of distinct reservations. He had nothing against Kinsolving's engineering ability. The man's ratings had been the highest. But he had been too steeped in the drivel poisoning the schools on Earth.

Give in to the aliens. Don't make them mad. Fit into a tiny niche and pick up their crumbs. Soon enough mankind would be allowed to join in. Soon. Very soon.

Humbolt snorted and rubbed his nose. He didn't accept such a passive philosophy for an instant. Not after he'd heard the Plan.

Humbolt opened his eyes and rocked slightly to one side. He idly punched up Kinsolving's file. He shook his head. Along with the ability to squeeze more ore from Deepdig number two than any other engineer employed by IM went a certainty that bordered on monomania. The man's stubbornness once he thought he was right was without limit.

His nose twitched again. Humbolt rubbed it, then jumped out of his chair when a soft, oily voice said, "There are drugs that might alter his opinions."

"What?" Humbolt's hand sank into the folds of his jacket to touch the handle of a stun rod. His eyes narrowed when he saw the overdressed man who had managed to enter the room, circle behind him and watch unobserved for—how long?

The man smiled disarmingly and held out his

hands to silently proclaim himself harmless. Humbolt almost accepted that. The man's clothing bordered on the absurd. Soft pinks and mint greens melted in formless swirls on a silk doublet with frilled white lace cuffs. The collar hung open to reveal a dozen platinum- and diamond-studded necklaces, any of which would have looked better around a woman's neck. Tight black stretch breeches with a codpiece and calf-high leather boots turned a parody of fashion into an outright joke

But Humbolt didn't laugh. Something about the man's eyes warned him this would be dangerous. And his unannounced visitor had entered without tripping any of the alarms Humbolt had planted for security.

"The alarms, good sir?" the man said in his unctuous voice. "Is that the point worrying you so?"

"Those were the best IM has. They didn't malfunction."

"But of course not." The man smiled, showing perfect white teeth rimmed in gold with occasional diamond, ruby and emerald embeddings. "I must caution those on the board of directors about this model." From nowhere the man produced one of the alarms. He tossed it casually onto the table.

"Who are you? You're not with the company."

An even wider smile almost dazzled Humbolt. For the first time, true fear stabbed at his heart. His knuckles turned white as he tensed on the handle of the stun rod.

"Of course I am."

"I'm a director. I know all the company personnel on Deepdig."

"Yes, you are a director, good sir." The man moved with fluid grace and settled daintily into a chair in front of Humbolt's desk. Foppishly crossing his legs and smoothing nonexistent wrinkles in his black breeches, the man asked, "Do you think this codpiece is too, well, too much? I was torn between its more daring fashion statement and modesty. I chose the former, of course. Never hesitate to be yourself, eh? But your opinion is of some importance, Mr. Humbolt."

Humbolt sank back into his chair and tapped the indent-key on the computer console. The screen blinked instantly, signalling a null match.

"Company records show you're not an employee, but no one except Interstellar Materials' personnel is allowed on planet. That's part of our agreement with the Lorr."

"You're asking how I came to this rather out-of-the-way spot?" The man fluffed his collar ruffles and smiled. This time the expression chilled Humbolt completely.

He wasn't sure even his weapon would be enough against this dandy. And he didn't know why he felt that. Becoming director of IM hadn't been easy. He had killed along the way—and worse.

Kenneth Humbolt wasn't sure even his quick reflexes would be enough. And he didn't know why. Uncertainty always worried him. Sweat began beading on his forehead.

"Is it too warm for you? Oh, pardon me. I am so rude at times. You are just in from GT 4. A chilly place, that, and not one I care for. Warmer climes are better suited for living though the cooler ones afford greater opportunity for displaying a well-developed ... wardrobe."

The man gestured and Humbolt almost froze. The simple pass of a hand had caused the thermostat to drop to its lowest setting.

"How'd you get here?" Humbolt asked again.

"How do you get the ore off Deepdig?" the man riposted. "We need not concern ourselves with trivial matters. My time is valuable, and I am ever so sure yours is, also. Am I correct in this, Mr. Humbolt?"

Humbolt's shoulders rippled as he jerked out the stun rod, finger pressing the firing stud before the weapon had even cleared its holster. The back of the chair where the man had been exploded, splinters flying everywhere.

The man stood beside Humbolt, thumb and forefinger lightly touching Humbolt's wrist.

"Drop the stun rod, Mr. Humbolt," he said, the hint of true amusement dancing on his too-handsome features. Dark-painted eyes gleamed with a feral cruelty. Humbolt twitched, then screamed. The thumb and forefinger grip tightened with steely intensity.

"Stop it!" Humbolt shrieked. "You're breaking my wrist!"

"Oh, sorry, Mr. Humbolt. It wouldn't do to damage you, would it? Your services are of considerable importance to IM." As if brushing off an insect, the man pushed Humbolt's wrist away.

"You're Villalobos', aren't you?" Humbolt demanded. "You're Cameron."

"I do confess to the latter, Mr. Humbolt." Cameron made a broad, mocking bow as if he paid obeisance to some Earthly king of a dozen centuries earlier. "But to state that I somehow belong to Dr. Villalobos is wrong. I work tirelessly for IM, as you do. Maria happens to be my immediate superior, that's all."

"Maria?" Humbolt had never heard anyone use Villalobos' first name so casually. The small, dark director was more commonly referred to as "that bitch."

Cameron's laugh carried true scorn in it. Humbolt couldn't decide whether it was scorn for Villalobos or himself.

"The good lady's relationship is special to me in

ways other than that of employer—employee, but then yours is special with her, also, is it not?"

Humbolt would gladly break her spine and leave her paralyzed for the rest of her natural life if he could.

"Yes, we share a special rapport," Humbolt said. He straightened in the chair and forced himself to keep from rubbing his still-hurting wrist. "Why are you on Deepdig? IM business, of course, but what? I was not informed."

Cameron made a dismissing gesture with his hand. "An oversight, I am sure. The bureaucratic nightmare on GT 4 will drown us all in trivia and misplaced orders one day."

"You are here under my command?"

A slight sneer rippled along Cameron's lips. "But of course! How can it be any other way? You, after all, are a director and I am only a lowly paid employee."

"How did you circumvent the alarm system?"

"My knowledge is extensive when it comes to robot devices. The alarm system can be thought of as disembodied sensors for a robot. I merely approached it in that fashion and, not wanting to disturb you while you were so hard at work, entered and waited to be noticed."

Humbolt reached out tentatively for the stun rod. Cameron made no move to prevent it. Humbolt almost jerked it back across the desk. Cameron paid no attention to the furtive movement. Humbolt felt as if the assassin had dismissed him completely as a threat; primping and smoothing his costume ranked higher.

"Why are you here?"

Cameron looked up, long eyelashes almost fluttering. The glint of sunlight coming through a skylight caught an emerald mounted in a front tooth and reflected away, almost blinding Humbolt.

"You must learn to be more diplomatic in your queries," Cameron chided. "It seldom pays to rush forward without knowing the exact nature of the terrain."

"I have work to do. Why did Villalobos send you to Deepdig?"

"Dr. Villalobos is my immediate superior," Cameron said, "but she did not send me. Chairman Fremont did."

Humbolt forced himself to stay silent. Anything he said now would be wrong. He couldn't show weakness, indecision, any hint of vacillation. If Fremont distrusted him and sent a watchdog to report the slightest mistake, it might be necessary to arrange an accident for the spy. How he would do that conveniently escaped Humbolt at the moment. Cameron's reputation hardly seemed credible, but Humbolt faced him and sensed more than the fop in him.

Without realizing he did so, Humbolt rubbed his injured wrist.

"Come along, Mr. Humbolt. I have a small demonstration prepared just for your benefit." The way Cameron spoke turned the request into a knife-edged order.

"I have work to do. Kinsolving is a problem that must be—"

"Supervisor Kinsolving is *my* problem now, Mr. Humbolt. Chairman Fremont has decided that the psychological profile on the man indicates that we lavish attention on him exceeding that of which you are capable."

Humbolt felt the storm clouds of anger mounting.

"It has been deemed best that you not dirty your hands with such minor matters. Allow me to do my task, then leave. Keeping the Lorr pacified and Deepdig open to IM exploitation is paramount. The Plan must be served."

"The Plan *will* be served," Humbolt said bitterly.

Cameron stood and walked on silent feet to the door. Humbolt didn't see how the man did it but the door slid back without Cameron touching the opener. Humbolt tucked the stun rod into its holster and hurried after Cameron. The assassin walked with a deceptively easy step, his long legs covering more ground than Humbolt could comfortably match without almost doubling his own stride.

"Where are we going?" Humbolt still had a mental picture of Fremont raging against Humbolt and how the Lorr had taken control of the situation—and Fremont ordering the elimination of those he considered responsible.

"Not far. There. See the Bizzie?"

Humbolt nodded.

"Don't worry. The agent-general won't miss this one. It is a ... derelict."

The alien hunkered down, glaring at them with those haunting, pupilless eyes. Fingers like tentacles wove intricate patterns Humbolt interpreted as obscene gestures.

Cameron barked something in the Lorr tongue that made the Bizarre jump to his feet and run like the wind.

"The study of Bizzie languages has been a minor hobby for some time," Cameron explained. "It is always proper to study your enemy, to learn all you can of him before destroying him."

"What are you going to do?"

"Robots," Cameron went on, paying no attention to Humbolt. "Robots are not a hobby with me. They are my life. They can achieve perfection in their limited universe. It is that perfection which draws me the most strongly. For instance, the Bizzie has been promised his life if he can escape."

"You can't kill him!" protested Humbolt. "If the agent-general learns about this—"

"The Lorr will never find this one. See how he dodges and runs." Cameron's voice became cold and tinted with a hatred that made Humbolt take an involuntary step away. "Those boneless legs will soon cease their rush away. No human could match the Bizzie's speed or endurance. But my friend is not human."

A soft hum filled the air. Humbolt spun and saw a small robot floating on a repulsor field a meter to his left. Small ceramic plates turned on mobile bases and a whip antenna fluttered behind the tubular body like a dog's tail.

"Surface acoustic wave sensors," said Cameron. "Those plates. They pick up the Bizzie's scent a thousand times better than the keenest bloodhound. Even without the other sensing devices—mostly of my own design—the SAWS could follow a single Bizzie—or human—through the most crowded city on the most crowded planet."

"And?" prompted Humbolt, fascinated in spite of himself. Cameron silently handed over a pair of goggles. Humbolt donned them and blinked at the unexpected view. Focusing at the end of his nose gave the countryside as seen by the robot. Focusing farther gave him normal vision. A sudden rush staggered him.

"It requires practice," Cameron said, mocking him. "Watch carefully."

Humbolt brought his eyes in close and saw everything that the robot hunter did. In less than a minute it had weaved in and out of rocks and scrubby trees and gone across a stream to find the alien. The Lorr died horribly within five seconds of the robotic attack.

Cameron removed the goggles from Humbolt's head and tucked them away in the voluminous folds of his blouse. "Remarkable, isn't it?"

"What's the purpose of showing me this?"

Surprise crossed Cameron's face. "Why, I thought you would enjoy seeing a Bizzie destroyed. One less for the Plan."

"That's all?"

Cameron laughed. "That's all. Now I must attend to business. Chairman Fremont has requested my immediate presence back on GT 4—bringing back the sad news that Supervisor Kinsolving has died an accidental death."

Cameron said nothing more. He left in a haze of pastel silks and flashing black-clad legs. Humbolt watched until the killer vanished in the serene countryside. Humbolt pitied Barton Kinsolving. The man was a good engineer and might have been an asset for IM if his profile had only shown a greater acceptance for the divine destiny of mankind.

The Plan would be served. No matter who died, the Plan would be served.

CHAPTER SIX

EVERYWHERE HE TURNED Barton Kinsolving ran into a Lorr agent-captain. They insisted on prying into every nook and cranny of the mine until no work was being done. Kinsolving resigned himself to letting the aliens do their job. He didn't like it, but he knew that the sooner they satisfied themselves, the sooner they would leave.

Kinsolving went into his office and sank into the wheezing pneumatic chair. He moved around uncomfortably, aware that the chair failed to match his contours in several places. Like everything else, the chair refused to do its job properly. He sighed and tried to get it all straight in his mind.

Kinsolving wasn't sure that he did a good job. Since the disaster with the robominer and the flooding of the lower levels, nothing had gone as it should.

Ala Markken. Kinsolving went numb inside thinking of her. How he loved her. How he *had* loved her. Kinsolving worried over the confusion he felt. Just because he had found that she'd stolen a considerable amount of ore from Interstellar Materials didn't make him love her any less, but she had tried to kill him. The man found that almost impossible to believe, yet the facts were obvious.

Ala had been in charge when the robot miner had lasered into the underground river. This Kinsolving pushed aside. It might have been an accident or Ala might have done it deliberately to hide the massive ore thefts. With waters raging almost two kilometers under the surface, anything seemed believable. Kinsolving smiled wanly. The Lorr agent-general might have even believed that a considerable amount of ore had been lost.

Kinsolving's smile tightened. The ore on level nineteen had been lifted. And the same heavy-lifter had been dropped down the elevator shaft in an attempt to crush him.

Ala Markken. She had done it. His lover had tried to kill him.

"You. Human one. Where are the assay reports?" came a harsh demand.

Kinsolving looked up, eyes misted with the impact of Ala's deliberate actions. "What?"

"It is required that we obtain assay reports for each level, for each vein of ore. They are not in your files."

Kinsolving stared at the Lorr, then heaved himself to his feet. He went to a slave-station computer the alien could use and banged in the access code. The information flashed on the screen. "This is it. We put it in the same database as the personnel records. Much the same format, saves space and time and—"

"Your alibis are of no importance to me." The Lorr swiveled on his crazy-hinged knees and stalked out.

Kinsolving's anger mounted, then faded. Officious, rude bureaucrats were the least of his worries. In his graduate school's required xeno culture and psychology class he had been taught that the aliens resented mankind's venturing to the stars, but that this attitude could be overcome. Not easily, not quickly, but their confidence and cooperation could be won. Sometimes he wondered.

"To hell with them," he said. Why should the Lorr be different from human auditors? He had the same problems when IM sent out their fleet of nameless, gnomelike accountants.

Kinsolving frowned. IM audited the mine records once every planetary year. Ala had been on-planet for four years. How had she hidden the discrepancy between lifting from the mine and lifting from the planet's surface? Kinsolving pulled the master console closer to his desk and began examining the records to find some clue. Several times he found a block on the records; the Lorr shut him off.

But the evidence of how Ala had stolen so much ore—and where she had sent it—remained a mystery.

Idly, Kinsolving punched up the woman's personnel record. Her lovely oval face stared at him from the screen. Almost savagely, he punched the Cancel button. Without knowing it, Kinsolving requested his own files and found his own likeness staring out at him.

As mine supervisor, Kinsolving had access to all personnel records but he had never taken the time to examine his own. He did his job, he got good raises and promotions and that was enough for him. He took pride in his work and what difference did it make what had been entered on his company files?

He examined them now. And he was not certain he agreed with the IM psychologist's appraisal. Then Kinsolving chuckled.

"Stubborn to a fault, recalcitrant, complete self-assurance, that's me," he decided. He frowned when he found a special flag at the end of the record. Working for a few minutes to access the corresponding tag file resulted in repeated Entry Denied warnings flashing on the screen. Kinsolving hunched forward and worked in earnest to break into this area of the database.

He was the supervisor. He should be able to see all the records. An hour of futile effort hadn't diminished his curiosity or determination, but Kinsolving slowly came to the realization that the tag had been put on his file back on Gamma Tertius 4 and no corresponding entry existed in the mine's database.

None of the other personnel records carried a similar flag, and this made Kinsolving all the more determined to find what IM thought of him—and wanted kept from prying eyes.

He glanced up when one of his few remaining workers poked his head inside the office door.

"Mr. Kinsolving?"

"What is it, Mac?"

"Don't know for sure. Getting odd readings from deep in the mine. Level nineteen. I ran a foptic probe and didn't find anything."

Kinsolving knew the limits of the fiber optic probes mounted on robotic surveyors. Not every frequency of visible light was transmitted since their primary use was detecting underground hot spots and areas of cold where water might run—rivers such as the one Ala Markken had ordered the robominer to drill into.

"How odd?" Kinsolving asked. "Anything to endanger the equipment?"

"Could be," the man said. Kinsolving knew he'd have to pry every bit of information from McClanahan. He was the most junior of those remaining and felt inadequate for the job he assumed.

Kinsolving didn't want to tell the man that he *was* inadequate, that his training and temperament were not suited to direct an entire shift. But Deepdig number two ran shorthanded because of Ala and the others. Even if valuable automated equipment hadn't been lost, Kinsolving would have been hardpressed to keep the mine operating at nominal capacity.

"Gas indications? More damp readings?" Kinsolving asked.

"Weirder than that. I know those indicators. You want to take a look at the board?"

Kinsolving rose silently and followed McClanahan to the control center. They passed two Lorr on the way. Each group pointedly ignored the other. Kinsolving swung into the command chair and scanned the console. Most of the indicators showed normal readings, but one flashed a slow, deliberate purple.

"You're right. This isn't usual." Ala Markken might have recognized the signal, but Kinsolving didn't. He punched up a Help on the screen and read it twice. "Never seen this before," he told McClanahan. "I'm going down. This shows that we hit a pocket of radon gas, but that's not possible. Not in this ore structure. And all we have mounted on the robominers are Geiger counters. I don't see any way we could get this indication."

"You mean it's showing radon gas but we don't have any equipment to detect it?"

"That's it. I'm afraid this might be a malfunction in the detector circuitry."

"But I checked that, first thing," the man protested. "All came out normal within limits."

Kinsolving shrugged. When working almost two kilometers underground, only one level above a flooded network, anything was possible. One piece of equipment failing in this manner might indicate bigger problems brewing in the bowels of the mine.

More problems were the last thing Kinsolving needed.

"We don't have time to pull it from the stoop and get it back up the shaft to examine. Keep the robot working. I'll assume manual control at the shaft, turn it off and then check it out."

"Manual overrides my controls, right?" McClana-han didn't sound happy about this.

"Safety measure. You know that. Where's the tool kit? Good, there it is." Kinsolving picked up the pack containing spare block circuits and other control components. With luck he could be down in the mine, fix the problem and return before the end of the shift.

"I can do that, if you want, Mr. Kinsolving," the man offered.

Kinsolving considered this offer seriously. He had no lingering traces of claustrophobia in spite of being trapped at the bottom of the mine. He felt *comfortable* in mine shafts. But more than this, he didn't want McClanahan shutting down the robo-miner. The only job the young man did worse than running the control console was repair work.

"Thanks, but I'll see to it. I'll take a com-link. Keep in touch. If anything more goes wrong, let me know right away."

"Yes, sir."

Kinsolving hefted the pack containing the repair parts and went to the head of the shaft. He stood and stared at the open cage for a moment, then entered. A deep breath, a slightly shaking hand touching the level eighteen button and he plummeted into the bowels of the planet.

"You there, Mac?" he asked, toggling his com-link.

"Here, sir. No problems. No more problems, I should say. Atmosphere levels normal, no damp, nothing but the robominer's radon indication."

"I'll wear a respirator," Kinsolving told him. "That won't pose much of a problem communicating."

"Muffles your voice, that's all," McClanahan said.

Kinsolving fitted the bulky head gear onto his face, hung the com-link at his belt and stepped out on level eighteen. The throb of pumps working on the lowest levels came to him as vibrations through his boot soles. Almost half of all his robot equipment strove to clean out the bottom four levels. He couldn't afford to have even one robominer on the upper levels out of commission.

Setting his hand flash, Kinsolving walked briskly along the stoop, the walls brushing either shoulder and occasional ceiling protrusions causing him to duck. By the time he reached the end of the stoop where the robominer's laser sizzled and popped and worked on the ore vein, Kinsolving scooted along on hands and knees.

He used the com-link controls to deactivate the robominer. Using his flash, he examined the immediate area. It appeared no different from any other vein found in the mine. He knew trapped pockets of any gas wouldn't be visible, but he saw no reason to expect the chemically inert radioactive gas in this strata. The 57–71s weren't usually found in sands containing thorium or pitchblende or even coal. He had studied the geologist's report and no radium had been found.

The detector on the robot had to be faulty. There was no other explanation.

The rock where the laser had been directed cooled enough to allow Kinsolving to slide forward. He touched the back of the robominer's metallic carapace. No heat. That meant the internal equipment probably functioned properly. Kinsolving opened the repair hatch and shone his light inside. All internal readouts were normal.

"Mac, you there?" he called, toggling the com-link.

"Yes, sir. Find something?"

"When was this unit in the repair shop last?"

"Routine maintenance over three months ago, sir. The lasing chamber had developed a leak and we had to replace the tube. Nothing else detected then."

"Someone's been inside. Bright scratches on the inner casing where a board has been replaced recently." Kinsolving knew that the robominer's normal operation would have oxidized those scratches in less than a week. Someone had tampered with the warning circuits—within the past day or two.

He pulled the suspect board, leaving new scratches on the robot's casing. Kinsolving plugged it into a portable tester and watched the readings. One after another blinked green until he came to one of a dozen circuits that weren't operational in this model robominer.

"Someone's added a false warning," he told McClanahan. He got no immediate response. "Mac? You still there? Mac!"

"Sir, get the hell out of there. I'm getting bad readings all over level eighteen. Vibration. The strain gauges show the roof is collapsing!"

Kinsolving didn't need the remote warning. The walls trembled and dust began to fall, obscuring vision for more than a few meters. Kinsolving started to crawl back to the larger part of the stoop, then stopped. His flash beam hit the wall of billowing dust and cut him off from seeing more than an arm's length now. The rumbles told the real story, however.

Kinsolving flopped over onto his back, got to the robominer and activated it. Red lights flared inside, indicating that he hadn't reinstalled the warning circuits. He didn't care. The robot would work without those boards. He manually programmed it to reverse the direction of its cutting laser, then started it to work.

The coherent beam snapped into existence just centimeters above his head. Kinsolving pressed close to the metallic side of the robominer and worked around it as the machine began to trace its way back toward the elevator shaft. The laser drilled a hole through dust and debris and afforded a better view than he could have hoped for without it.

Less than ten meters from the shaft and the elevator that would get him to the surface, the roof collapsed. Kinsolving choked, as the shockwave of dust and stony fragments momentarily forced away all the air from the mouth of his respirator filter.

He shone his flash against the solid wall. To dig through it with his bare hands would be impossible. Kinsolving started the robominer cutting. He hoped it would break through before another tremor brought down all those tons of rock on his head.

He sat and watched and waited, unable to do anything more except worry.

CHAPTER SEVEN

BARTON KINSOLVING longed to reach over to the
working robominer and turn up the cutting laser's
power. He held back. The trapped air in the stoop
had turned stale quickly. To increase the robominer's cutting speed would reduce the oxygen in
the air even more. Kinsolving sat and wheezed and
wondered what had gone wrong this time.

After all, Ala Markken was in the Lorr prison.
She couldn't be responsible for a second attempt on
his life.

Kinsolving came to the gloomy conclusion that
mining, in spite of the almost total automation, was
still a dangerous business.

"Sir?" The com-link crackled with static. "You
there, Mr. Kinsolving?"

"Still here, Mac," he said, not wanting to use any
more oxygen than necessary. "What happened?"

"Lost you for a minute. Getting a spotty signal."

Kinsolving didn't answer. McClanahan would get
to the point in his own time. Kinsolving hoped he'd
be around to hear it.

"You there, Mr. Kinsolving? I got readings of severe vibration. The computer analysis is that some
damn fool was blasting in a stoop running parallel
to the one you're in. Too much explosive and weak-
ened supports from the flooding caused the roof collapse." A long pause with almost deafening static,
then, "You there, Mr. Kinsolving?"

"I'm here," Kinsolving said. He sat with his arms locked around his knees, thinking hard. Another attempt on his life. Blasting on this level hadn't been approved for almost eight months. The laser cutters worked faster and better once the first tunnel had been opened. Why weaken the stoops with dangerous explosives when the robominer's operation cut through the heart of the ore vein and left a fused tunnel stronger than the uncut rock?

If it wasn't Ala who tried to kill him this time, who could it be?

The only answer possible made Kinsolving furious. When he got out, he'd find Kenneth Humbolt and snap his neck.

Kinsolving looked up to see the robominer's readouts showing a decreasing power level. He started to take the chance and increase cutting power when he noticed the reason for the slowing. Sonic probes measured the distance to the far side of the rock fall. The robot was within centimeters of breakthrough.

"This can't be right," Kinsolving said aloud. His breath momentarily fogged the inner lenses of the respirator. He waited for a clearing, then checked the robominer. It had bored through only six meters of rock. By his estimate another four meters remained.

A sudden rush of air caused dust to swirl around him. He squinted as he looked into a powerful hand flash.

"You all right, Kinsolving?" came a voice he knew too well.

"I'm fine," he answered. Kinsolving turned off the robominer and gingerly picked his way over the still-hot, lasered rock. He tumbled out to find himself sitting at Humbolt's feet. The man helped Kinsolving to his feet and started brushing him off.

"That's all right, Humbolt," he said brusquely. "I'll get cleaned up after we're out of the mine."

"I thought we'd lost you," said Humbolt, slapping Kinsolving on the back. "Glad to see you're still alive."

"Why are you here?"

Humbolt tipped his head and peered at Kinsolving. "You sound suspicious. Hell, Barton, I just *rescued* you. Oh, you'd have cut your way out in a while, but you're out in less than half the time it'd have taken your unit."

"Thanks. But what are you doing here?" Kinsolving refused to be mollified.

"I returned to the compound just as the quake hit. I heard your McClanahan and figured you needed help. Been a long time since I've been in a mine. I got my start in the field and, well, I decided to give you a hand."

"You ran a robominer from this side?"

"They haven't changed much," Humbolt said with some pride.

"It wasn't a quake," said Kinsolving.

Kinsolving watched Humbolt's expression. If he hadn't been studying the IM director carefully he would have missed the quickly passing cloud of anger. Humbolt knew it wasn't a natural quake; he knew this was no accident. But if Humbolt had orchestrated the new disaster, why bother rescuing the victim?

"You saved me another hour trapped back there," said Kinsolving. "Again, thank you." He didn't offer his hand, nor did Humbolt seem to expect the gratitude to extend that far.

"Let's get back to the surface. Your Mr. McClanahan can keep these robots busy from the control center. How long before they can be producing ore again?"

"Cleanup for this level will be minimal," said

Kinsolving, the engineer in him rising to the surface and hiding the suspicious, paranoid part of his nature. "If we keep at it—no letup on the night shifts—the stoop will be producing again within a day or two. Might need to shore up the roof. One robominer is adequate for that. The other can burrow back and find the vein."

"A day?" said Humbolt. "Good. I'll expect a report at the end of the week."

The elevator came to a smooth halt at the surface. Kinsolving ran from the cage and fell to the ground in appreciation for being free of a mine shaft that had for a second time almost been his grave. He sheepishly looked at Humbolt, embarrassed at this display of relief. But the director had already left the compound, walking briskly to a waiting vehicle. Even before Kinsolving could call out, the repulsor field of the vehicle hummed to life and it surged into the distance.

Kenneth Humbolt was in a hurry to get somewhere.

But where? Kinsolving wanted to know this as much as he wanted to know who had been responsible for the explosion in the mine. If it had been Humbolt, he saw no reason for the director to abruptly change his mind and rescue his victim.

"Mac, what's the status below?" he asked as he entered the control center. The young man bent over the console, working furiously.

"Got things programmed. Might be able to get ore production to nominal by this time tomorrow. Not much damage to the shaft or stoops." McClanahan's expression turned grim. "It was almost as if the explosion was meant to trap only you, Mr. Kinsolving."

He didn't bother telling McClanahan about the circuit board that had been tampered with. The spurious reading had been a lure. When he had descended the explosives had been detonated.

"Can you handle it, Mac? I've got to find Humbolt."

"Haven't seen him. You might try in town at the agent-general's office. Think I heard someone say he was there this afternoon for another hearing. But you'd know that, wouldn't you?"

"Right, Mac. I'd know all about that."

With grim determination, Barton Kinsolving went to his quarters, washed and changed his clothing, then went hunting for Humbolt. If the director had been scheduled to meet with the Lorr agent-general, what had brought him to the mine so unexpectedly—and at such an opportune time to save Kinsolving?

By the time he reached the suite of rooms he'd taken as an office while on Deepdig, Kenneth Humbolt was in a rage. He stormed into the room and bellowed to a robutler, "Get me Cameron! Get him now!"

"There's no need to be so upset, Director Humbolt," came the silky smooth voice from across the room. Humbolt spun and faced Cameron. The assassin sat in a chair, one lavender-colored linen-encased leg dangling indolently over the low arm. He smoothed back a vagrant strand of his sandy hair and patted it into place. All Humbolt saw were the heavy gold rings on the hand.

"Do you like this?" Cameron asked. "I had thought the Lorr lacking in even the basics of fashion, but I found this interesting cloth and had a rather good tailor make it into this for me." He held out his arms and displayed a forest green shirt with gold and silver highlights glinting in it. Large silver buttons with an eagle stamped in the metal paraded up the front to add contrast to the shirt.

"Why did you try to kill Kinsolving?" demanded Humbolt. "I don't care about your damned clothing. Why did you try to kill my mine supervisor?"

"I thought the matter had been settled, Director." Cameron swung his leg off the chair arm and lounged back, strong fingers tented just under his chin. "Do you think I would look more dashing with a beard? Nothing ostentatious, mind you. Just a small goatee?"

"Damn your facial hair!" shrieked Humbolt. Fists clenched, Humbolt forced control on himself. Only when he had regained control did he continue. "Answer me. Why did you try to kill Kinsolving?"

"Director, you had been told that Fremont instructed me to handle matters as I saw fit. It was obvious that Kinsolving's removal facilitated much." Cameron's expression changed from mocking amusement to something harder. "Why did I *try* to kill him?"

"You failed. He's still alive," Humbolt said, revelling in the assassin's surprise and chagrin. "You failed. Villalobos' pet killer failed. How will that look to Fremont?"

"What happened? I had planned this carefully. The computer results showed a ninety-five percent confidence level of success." Cameron eyed Humbolt coldly. "You intervened. You did something to thwart my plan to carry out Chairman Fremont's wishes."

"I arrived just as your explosives went off." Humbolt heaved a deep breath. "It's been quite a few years since I've been down in a mine, but I haven't forgotten how to run a robominer."

"You dug him out."

"He would have been free within another hour, even without my aid. If I had never appeared, Kinsolving would still be alive."

"Impossible. The explosive would have collapsed the entire stoop."

"It didn't. And he had repaired the robominer in the stoop and aimed it at the rock fall."

"The air. It wouldn't have been sufficient."

"It was. Kinsolving is used to the conditions in a mine. He had a respirator with him. What else would you expect of a man going to investigate on anomalous radon leak?"

"The respirator shouldn't have been enough. It doesn't *supply* oxygen, does it?" Cameron rubbed a forefinger along the line of his jaw as he worried over the problem. "He can be removed in other ways that appear to be accidental."

"You are not listening, Cameron. Kinsolving will *not* be removed under any circumstance. When I arrived and heard of his...misfortune...I retrieved him."

Cameron eyed the director coldly.

"You work for Interstellar Materials," Humbolt said, now in control. "I need Kinsolving alive. I order you *not* to harm him. If you don't like it, take my orders to the chairman."

"Chairman Fremont has given me orders contrary to yours," Cameron said lightly. "Are you recommending that I ignore him?"

"I'm recommending that you allow me to do my job. A clumsy attempt to remove Kinsolving almost ruined my plans for him. The chairman won't have any complaints when I am finished on Deepdig. No one loyal to IM and adhering to the Plan will be dissatisfied."

"What is it you want from me, Director Humbolt?"

Humbolt felt a rush of excitement. Cameron would never be his pawn, not with players the caliber of Maria Villalobos in the game, but it would be possible to use Cameron to his benefit.

This time.

Humbolt smiled and went to his desk. Sitting down, he lounged back and stared up at the skylight, considering how best to phrase his orders. "Your talents will be required in less than a day, I am sure. It would be nice if you had a few of your tracking robots ready. I foresee extreme problems brewing at Deepdig number two." Humbolt smiled even more. "It might even be a new disaster for us."

"Supervisor Kinsolving dies?"

"Not at all. The Bizzies might have the wrong people jailed for tax evasion and the other tedious crimes against Lorr law. Wouldn't that be a shame?"

"Chairman Fremont, shall we say, *requested* that Barton Kinsolving be removed permanently. Our chairman feels that the man is a danger to the Plan."

"The Plan will prevail. And Barton Kinsolving will be in no position to harm either IM or the Plan. In fact, he will aid the Plan."

"What more can we ask, eh?" said Cameron.

"Nothing more. Prepare your equipment, Mr. Cameron. When everything comes together—soon—it will be needed in a hurry."

"It will be a true pleasure, Director, to demonstrate my expertise once again for the good of IM and the Plan."

Humbolt said nothing, his eyes flashing from the assassin to the door, giving Cameron a silent dismissal. He watched as the particolored fop strode across the room and vanished. Humbolt kept from laughing in relief, the nervous strain removed.

When he succeeded on Deepdig, perhaps he could find a way of using Cameron against Villalobos to permanently remove her as a director. Perhaps,

perhaps. Humbolt turned to finish last-minute preparations. Kinsolving was due at the prison soon, or so said the computer projections based on the man's personality. Kenneth Humbolt wanted everything to be ready when the mine supervisor arrived.

CHAPTER EIGHT

BARTON KINSOLVING needed to know. Nothing of the past few weeks made any sense to him. Life had been easy—good—before the mine accident, before Ala Markken had tried to kill him, before everything had fallen into ruin.

Kinsolving's anger rose and faded as he guided the car across the countryside. Being out of control wouldn't help. He had to keep his emotions in check and learn. *Learn,* he thought with some bitterness. He knew enough now to be upset and hurt. Finding out all the details might hurt even more. But not to know the truth would haunt him the rest of his life.

Ala loved him. He was sure of that. And he still loved her. It hadn't been easy for him to fall in love initially, and he now refused to stop in spite of all that had happened.

"Must be an explanation. Must be," he muttered over and over. With automatic skill, he drove until he saw the small city looming from the grassy prairie. The Lorr presence on Deepdig had never been great, and the size of the city proved this. Hardly more than ten thousand lived here, their duties primarily that of an overseer.

What else they did on Deepdig Kinsolving couldn't say. He had never been curious enough to ask before. Ten thousand aliens weren't needed to enforce mining regulations and tariffs. The rest must do something. Support? What support did the

Lorr require? A small shuttle field stood seven kilometers off to the east, but the repair facilities there were minimal. IM's workers outnumbered the Lorr two to one.

Kinsolving had driven past the prison building many times in his tenure on Deepdig but had never been inside. Now he idled the car and went up the steep steps not made for human legs. Kinsolving puffed and panted before he finished scaling them.

To the guard just inside the door he said, "I want to talk to a prisoner. Ala Markken."

"No visitors, human," the guard snapped.

Kinsolving had spent a lifetime dealing with petty functionaries. Alien or human didn't matter. They all thought in the same patterns, had the same concerns. Protecting their private power domains ranked highest in their universe and anyone challenging their authority was not only suspect but was the enemy.

"I need to speak with her. Can you help me with the proper procedure?" This got him noticed. Any appeal to superior ability—allowing the bureaucrat to function—got noticed.

"Down the corridor, to the left, to the left again. See the watch commander."

"Thank you, Lieutenant," Kinsolving said. He had no idea what the Lorr's rank might be, but he knew that an officer wouldn't be standing guard duty. The inflated rank inflated the guard's ego. He gruffly motioned Kinsolving into the depths of the prison.

Smiling slightly at this minor victory, Kinsolving knew it would be only a matter of waiting, patience and humoring the Lorr before he got to see Ala. Not for the first time Kinsolving silently thanked his professor in xeno relations for the tough semesters and the needed experience gained in dealing with aliens.

"Watch Commander?" Kinsolving asked.

The Lorr seated behind a desk that seemed more a single plank set on two sawhorses glared at him. Kinsolving repeated all he'd said before, offered to fill out the paperwork, complimented the alien repeatedly—and an hour later was shown into a small, bare cell where Ala Markken sat crosslegged on the floor.

"Ala!" he exclaimed. He bit back his outrage at the conditions until the watch commander had left. To complain would only worsen the woman's stay. "This is awful!"

She had been stripped to the waist and a solid steel chain fastened firmly about her middle. The end of the chain had been bolted into the wall. Ala could stand and move almost a meter before coming to the end of her bonds. Of sanitary facilities, Kinsolving saw none.

"First time to visit a Bizzie holding pen?" she asked. The anger and bitterness he'd expected were seriously absent.

"I'll try to get you some furniture—and free from the chain. God! They can't do this to you."

"It gets cold in here at night, being naked like this," she said, folding her arms over her breasts. "But there's nothing sexual about it. Not with the Lorr. They treat all their prisoners the same. That's what our treaty with them says."

"What about sanitary facilities. They must..."

"They let us use the facilities down the hall twice a day. I have to plan." She smiled weakly. "But then, what else do I have to do?"

"I'll do something. Get you out. There has to be bail. Why hasn't Humbolt bailed you out?"

"There's no bail in the Lorr legal system. Anyone arrested is assumed guilty, so why let loose preconvicted felons? Besides, darling Bart, I *have* been tried and convicted. You remember the trial?"

"There must be an appeal."

"We're dealing with Bizarres," she said. "We don't share the same criminal systems."

"You don't need to be insulting to them. This is all—it's a mistake. I'll take care of it."

"Why?" she asked, cocking her head to one side. Once-lustrous hair fell in grimy ropes and her face needed a good washing, but her eyes were still sharp and clear—and accusing. "You're talking to the woman who tried to kill you. I stole all that ore. I'm a desperate criminal, not your lover."

Kinsolving went to her, dropped to his knees and threw his arms around her. For an instant, she resisted, then relaxed and flowed against him as she always had before. Her body shook and salty tears dampened his shoulder. But when she pulled away, she had herself under control once more.

"Why are you here, Bart?"

"I love you. I don't know why you stole the ore. I don't even care."

"And trying to kill you?"

"Why, Ala? You must have had a reason. Explain it to me. Make me understand. I want to try."

She pushed entirely free of his arms and sat with her bare back pressed into the cold stone corner of the cell. Her dark eyes fixed on his and she said in an even voice, "You have so many endearing qualities. I *do* love you, Bart, but you can't understand. You just can't. It's not in you."

"Please."

She heaved a deep breath and her eyes dropped. "All right. You wondered what I did with the thousands of kilos of ore I pirated. It went off-planet on IM's regularly scheduled ships. I was ordered by IM to steal the rare earths."

"To avoid paying the Lorr their duties and severance taxes? But that's a minor expense compared with the benefit of the metals."

"I didn't expect you to understand." She heaved another deep sigh. "IM doesn't want the Bizzies to know how much we are really lifting. If they did, they'd close down the mines to prevent us from building more starships."

"What do the Lorr care?"

"Not just the Lorr. All the Bizarres. They want to hold Earth back. They want to keep us humans a second-rate race. But we won't let them. The extra samarium is going into stardrive engines they know nothing about. We'll expand and beat them at their own game!"

Ala's passion couldn't be denied. A flush tinted her cheeks, and her eyes now blazed with the fanaticism of a religious convert. One of the strongest influences on Kinsolving and his view of the universe came from Professor Delgado's xeno culture course. Everything he held to be an indisputable fact he heard Ala Markken denying.

"They're not evil." He looked at the way Ala was chained. "They just don't do things the way we do. Different histories, different ideas."

He paused when she didn't answer. "Why did you try to kill me?"

"Orders."

"From Humbolt?"

Ala nodded. Licking her lips and pulling her knees in close to her body, she said, "I didn't want to, Bart. You'll never know how hard it was for me to do it. Maybe that's why you're still alive. I...I unconsciously didn't do my best. I made mistakes that allowed you to live." She smiled a little and added, "I'm glad for that. If only you'd see it our way."

"So Humbolt shares your twisted view of the Lorr?"

"Of all aliens!" she flared. "You fool! They want to see us eradicated like vermin. I'm not going to let them. Oh, no, I won't let them! No one who believes in the Plan will!"

"The Plan?" he asked.

"Leave me alone. Go drain the mine. Do what you do best, Bart. Just don't come to see me again."

"What's this Plan?"

Ala Markken pulled her knees even tighter to her chest and rested her forehead on her knees. Kinsolving saw that she'd not speak to him again. He stood, heart threatening to explode in his chest. Calling for the watch commander and being let out of the cell, he left on putty-weak legs. Once, as he went down the corridor toward the alien's office, Kinsolving had to reach out and support himself. The watch commander swiveled on his strangely hinged knees and simply stared. Kinsolving failed to read any expression.

"Why do you keep her like that? Chained like an animal?"

"She is."

Kinsolving tried to hit the Lorr, but the alien's reflexes were far too fast. Kinsolving's fist missed by centimeters. The Lorr grabbed Kinsolving's wrist and jerked hard enough to send the human sprawling.

"Leave. Now. What the prisoner told you—believe it. Do not return here."

"You were listening!"

The Lorr pointed toward the door leading back the way Kinsolving had entered. Kinsolving got to his feet, even shakier than before, and obeyed the silent order. He ought to have realized that the Lorr would listen to any conversation. Ala was a prisoner and therefore denied all rights, even to common decency.

Kinsolving shook himself when he got outside. He couldn't judge the aliens by Earth standards. Most stargoing cultures treated criminals with more brutality than the Lorr. But in spite of Ala's order to never see her again, Kinsolving knew he wouldn't stop trying to free her. She had tried to kill him, she had robbed the Lorr of taxes—and he still loved her. He knew that a few weeks away from Humbolt and IM and Deepdig with him would work miracles. Ala Markken had been duped into this theft, possibly by Kenneth Humbolt.

And if not by Humbolt, then by others high up in IM's power structure. Kinsolving believed her when she said that the pilfered ore left Deepdig on IM freighters. The Lorr's surveillance satellite network around the planet would prevent any regular boosting of the rare earth oxides to pirate freighters.

Kinsolving refused to get back into his vehicle. Instead he walked the city streets aimlessly, trying to think, failing at it. Nothing came together properly in his mind. Kinsolving prided himself on logical, orderly thought processes. None of this seemed logical. Facts were missing. And Ala remained in prison.

Somehow Kinsolving's path took him to the solitary building where Kenneth Humbolt had established his office. He couldn't trust the IM director—not after Ala's revelation of the man's complicity and guilt—but he needed Humbolt's cooperation to free Ala. There was no other way.

Starting up the steps, Kinsolving paused and studied the street running perpendicular to the one he'd approached on. A large official Lorr vehicle was parked there. Two armed guards lounged against the fender, trading off-color jokes. Kinsolving shook his head. They might appear more birdlike than humans and have those bizarre amber, pupilless eyes but they were so similar in behavior.

Was he the only human who saw the similarities rather than the differences? What lies had Professor Delgado burned into his brain?

Kinsolving knew they weren't lies. Delgado had taught the truth, the only way that Earth might cfassume its place among the older, better established alien races.

Loud voices made Kinsolving hurry up the steps and slip inside the partially opened door, seeking the first refuge he could find. Just inside a sitting room he listened to the argument going on farther down the hall in the room Humbolt used for an office.

"It's proof, Agent-General. Look at it. Those six are innocent. They were nothing more than dupes."

"Following orders?" the Lorr demanded.

"They were ignorant. You have convicted the wrong ones. Examine the documents."

Kinsolving peered about and saw no one. On light feet he went to the opened office door and hazarded a quick glance inside. The Lorr agent-general stood swivelling to and fro on his universal joint knees, fingers rubbing along the side of the folder Humbolt had thrust across the desk.

"Why do you do this?"

"Interstellar Materials does not wish to see innocent employees punished. We have nothing but contempt for anyone stealing from you—and our company."

The agent-general nodded. Kinsolving saw that his final touch to the argument convinced the alien. Humans would steal from the Lorr, but they wanted revenge when humans stole from other humans. The logic appealed even to Kinsolving.

"We will examine these documents. If they reveal the data you claim, your six employees will be released and compensation delivered in accordance with our established procedures for such inequities."

"I am certain that IM will wish to contribute any such money to the Lorr to defray the loss caused by our thieving employee."

"That is another matter." The agent-general almost caught Kinsolving by surprise. Without a word of leave-taking, he swung about and started for the door. Not wanting to be caught spying, Kinsolving ducked down behind a table and pressed his sweaty back into the wall, trying to vanish. He succeeded enough that the Lorr stalked by him without even glancing down.

When the Lorr exited, Kinsolving heaved himself to his feet and went into Humbolt's office. He had never cared for the man, but if the director had evidence to free Ala Markken and the others, Kinsolving wanted to thank him.

Humbolt glanced up as Kinsolving entered, an expression mingling surprise and fear on his features.

"Supervisor," Humbolt said, almost stuttering, "I didn't expect you so soon."

"So soon?"

"I left a message for you with—what's his name? McClanahan. Yes, that's it. I told him to have you report here as soon as possible. But I just transmitted a code message. He's hardly had time to decipher, much less contact you."

"Code message? Did it have something to do with the evidence clearing Ala and the others?"

"Well, yes. Sit down, Kinsolving—Bart. This isn't easy for me, but please believe me when I say that IM has your best interests at stake in this sorry matter."

Kinsolving frowned. "What information could you give the Lorr to exonerate Ala?" She had confessed to Kinsolving. He knew she had committed the crimes.

"We decided to trade six employees for one. Wait!" Humbolt cried, holding up his hand when Kinsolving rocketed from the chair. "It's not like that at all. The documents I gave the Bizzie incriminate you.

That's true. As mine supervisor, you had the opportunity and means."

"You sold me out?"

"It means freeing Ala," Humbolt said, shrewdness in his every word.

"And letting me rot in their prison in her place!"

"Wait!" Humbolt's command froze Kinsolving. "Sit down and keep quiet. Time is important."

Kinsolving sat down, seething inside at the injustice.

"The Lorr needed someone to pin the blame on. They'd never allow Markken and the others to go free without finding a guilty party. The documents I handed over are fakes, but good ones. Ala Markken will be released; you will be the sole criminal in Lorr eyes."

"And?" asked Kinsolving, not knowing what to expect.

"And you will be long gone from Deepdig and far beyond Lorr justice. We're transferring you back to GT 4 immediately. There are other worlds requiring your special talents."

"How do you intend getting me there? The Lorr control access to Deepdig. Even more tightly now that this ore piracy has become known."

"We have a ship waiting at the spaceport right now for you. Go directly there and we'll boost you to a waiting speedster—it's mine."

"You'll tell the Lorr I stole it?"

"A nice touch." Humbolt tapped out a notation on his console. "That'll give even more credence to the story. You'll be back on GT 4, and Ala will join you soon."

"I don't like being made the scapegoat for all that's happened here. I know you ordered her to steal the oxides."

Humbolt's face hardened. "There is no other way

to free her. Or would you rather allow her to die in the Bizzie jail? She drew a forty-year sentence."

Kinsolving sat speechless. He'd never heard the sentence, just the guilty verdict. He couldn't allow Ala to spend forty years in such conditions.

"She tried to kill me," he said in a voice almost too low for Humbolt to hear.

"An unfortunate business, that," said Humbolt. "But you really have no other choice but to go directly to the spaceport. My scheme has been set into motion. The agent-general is not likely to believe me if I tell him the documents he has are all forgeries, not when it means a jail term for me. Forgery and lying to a Lorr senior field officer are both felonies."

"She'll be along soon?"

"Within a month or so," Humbolt assured him.

"I don't like this. I don't like my name being smeared."

"You'll like prison even less if you don't hurry. Go, Bart, go! Now!"

"Who do I contact?" Kinsolving asked.

"A man named Cameron. He's waiting for you," said Humbolt. The director rose and thrust out his hand. Hesitantly, Kinsolving shook it.

"Go. Hurry," urged Humbolt.

"Cameron?" asked Kinsolving, still unsure.

"Ask for no one else."

Kinsolving left at a run. It all made sense. Humbolt covered his part in the ore theft by pinning the blame on Kinsolving. But to IM it made no difference since if Ala was to be believed, the company ended up with all the rare earths. Kinsolving might even be greeted as a hero. The Lorr would have been thwarted and all IM personnel freed from their stinking jails.

But Barton Kinsolving still worried. He felt he was missing something.

CHAPTER NINE

BARTON KINSOLVING drove too fast, taking turns in the road with reckless abandon, but the pressure of time weighed heavily on him. He had misjudged Humbolt; the director actually cared about his employees. All his employees. Although Kinsolving didn't like being the one to carry the guilt for the thefts at the mine, he thought over Humbolt's scheme and decided it was workable.

The Lorr would never release Ala and the others without a bigger criminal in custody.

Kinsolving had to be that criminal.

He tensed as the vehicle skidded and ran over the edge of the roadway. For an instant the repulsor field faded when it failed to find the flat surface it expected. Auxiliary power cut in and held the vehicle up until Kinsolving wrestled it back onto the roadway. When the familiar hum returned and the whine vanished, he accelerated once more. He could have put it on automatic but the safety limiting circuits wouldn't have allowed such a breakneck pace.

Kinsolving trembled at the need to get away from Deepdig. The spaceport came up suddenly as he topped a low rise. The complex spread out for kilometers toward the east and north, most of it belonging to Interstellar Materials. Several of the stubby dark gray carbon-composite-hulled shuttles stood at the near side of the field, their blue and gold trident-and-star insignia gleaming in the pale sunlight.

Slowing slightly, Kinsolving guided the vehicle to a spot where the Lorr guards at the field wouldn't notice his approach. A dozen or more roads led into the field, most of them normally filled with heavy ore transports from the two rare earth mines. Those the Lorr guards checked for exit permits and tax stamps. Individual vehicles mattered little to them.

For that Kinsolving thanked his lucky stars.

He pulled up next to a corrugated shed and idled the vehicle. He wouldn't need it again. Kinsolving closed his eyes and mentally pictured the shuttle launch, the heavy pulsed laser beamed against the shuttle's underside splash plate, the entire vessel surging higher and higher until it reached orbit. From there it would be a matter of an hour or less to rendezvous with the speedster that had brought Humbolt from GT 4.

"Hey, you can't park there," came a querulous voice. "Move it or I'll dismantle the damn thing."

Kinsolving jerked, torn from his reverie. The mechanic approaching carried a small electronic circuitry work kit in one hand and a large torsion wrench in the other.

"You deaf?"

"I don't recognize you," Kinsolving said. "I'm supervisor at mine number two."

"Kinsolving?" the man asked, his attitude changing. "Sorry. I'm new here. Just got in a few days ago. Name's Cameron."

"You're the man I'm looking for," Kinsolving said, relief flooding through him. "Humbolt sent me."

"He did, eh?" Cameron smiled, his mouth flaring in the sunlight. Gold rimmed teeth and embedded reflecting gems made Kinsolving squint. Something about the mechanic made Kinsolving wary. His mouth alone carried more wealth than the vast majority of people on weary, worn Earth saw in a lifetime. But the manner more than the riches so ostentatiously displayed put Kinsolving on his guard.

"Do you know what's been happening at the mine?" he asked.

The mechanic smiled even broader and shook his head. "Don't care. I take my orders from the big boss. Whatever Mr. Humbolt says is law, far as I'm concerned."

This bothered Kinsolving even more. Cameron's tone mocked, as if he knew something that no one else did.

"Where's the shuttle? It's supposed to be ready for immediate takeoff."

"That one. See it? The one with the white steering fin?"

"I see it," Kinsolving said, "but it looks deserted. There's no activity in the firing pit." Before shuttle launch the heavy lasers required massive amounts of liquid nitrogen coolant. The plumes of condensation were vented to either side of the shuttle. During launch the plumes became so thick it appeared that the shuttle had developed a rocket thrust kicking up dust. Only when the vessel reached an altitude of a few hundred meters did the illusion vanish.

"Told to keep everything quiet. You running from something?" Cameron cocked his head to one side, as if listening for more than Kinsolving's reply.

"Just follow Mr. Humbolt's orders."

"Will do. Start hiking. By the time you get there, the pilot'll be anxious to push the launch button." Cameron pointed with the end of the wrench. Kinsolving started walking, only looking back when he'd gone a few paces.

Cameron had vanished into the building. On impulse, Kinsolving reversed his path, stopping just outside the door. From inside he heard Cameron's voice plainly.

"Is it wrong to obey the law, Agent-Captain?"

"No," came a Lorr's deep voice. "But why do you insist on obeying *our* law? This fugitive might have escaped. Are you a traitor to your own kind?"

Cameron laughed. "No sir, nothing like that." Kinsolving winced at the viciousness carried in those words. "But Director Humbolt ordered us all to obey your law to the letter. Said we've had enough trouble, and he wants to smooth out relations between the company and you ... people."

"Shuttle twenty-three is the fugitive's destination?"

"That's right. You can pick him up easily enough. He took off walking. Be a good ten minutes to get to the shuttle."

"When is your shuttle due to launch?"

Cameron laughed louder. "Not for a week or more. Got a busted steering vane and a fused control circuit that looks like glass. Couldn't lift if it had to."

Kinsolving looked around frantically. Cameron had betrayed him. Or had it been Humbolt? His mind raced, tiny pieces that had troubled him falling into a more coherent picture. Other than Humbolt's arrival weeks ago, there hadn't been any new IM personnel grounding on Deepdig. Cameron couldn't have just come in, as he claimed. And Kinsolving knew most of the ground crew by name and the rest by sight from his many trips here to ferry the ore into orbit.

It had to be Humbolt who betrayed him. He'd ordered him to seek out Cameron.

Kinsolving ran to the vehicle and powered it up. If shuttle twenty-three wasn't the one for him, another would do. Get off Deepdig, get into orbit, hijack Humbolt's speedster and get away. Back on GT

4 things would look different. Humbolt might try to throw him to the Lorr in exchange for Ala Markken and the others, but Kinsolving thought he might be able to follow the spurious plan—and still come out a free man.

The vehicle powered up, Kinsolving shoved the throttle forward to the maximum position. Acceleration slammed him into the cushions and caused a cloud of dust to rise from the tarmac. He rotated about the vehicle's vertical axis as he changed direction and headed for the far side of the launch field. The telltale plumes of nitrogen liquid turning to vapor came from beneath shuttle seventeen.

But Kinsolving's heart turned into ice when he saw that the shuttle didn't prepare for liftoff. Technicians worked on the launch laser, testing its cooling system.

"Hey, McKenna!" Kinsolving called to the head technician. "Are any of the shuttles ready to go up?"

The woman peered up from her work. "Hi, Bart. Can't say any are. Humbolt's been riding us hard about routine maintenance ever since he grounded. Won't be a launch for another week. You needing to get into orbit?"

"Right now," he said. The woman brushed back dark hair shot with strands of gray and shook her head.

"No time soon. We do have a small shuttle to reach Humbolt's speedster if he needs it. But it'll take about six hours to launch."

"Not good enough," he said.

"What's the hurry?"

"Too many problems," he said. "Say, do you know anything about the new mechanic? Cameron's his name."

"Cameron? Never heard of him. Or do you mean Carmen? She's over in shipping." The woman smiled. "She's still got it bad for you. She'd like nothing better than to console you about Ala."

"Can't a man have any secrets in this place?" he said with mock anger. The sound of sirens turned him cold inside. "Got to run."

"Bart, wait. Are they coming after you? We can hide you in the laser pit."

"Can't stay. If they ask after me, tell them everything." Kinsolving slammed the throttle forward again. He didn't want to get McKenna or any of her crew in trouble with the Lorr. That the aliens were racing across the tarmac with sirens blaring showed that they were on his trail.

"Not much of a trail," he muttered to himself as he weaved in and out of buildings and idled shuttles. Kinsolving worked at the wheel with grim concentration, but the Lorr inexorably narrowed the distance between vehicles. The fleeing human found himself circling about and returning to the same building where he'd met Cameron.

A new determination filled Kinsolving. He'd never be able to elude the Lorr. Out on this prairie they could see him for kilometers and kilometers. But he might have a few minutes before they caught him.

Those few minutes might be well spent beating the truth out of Cameron. The pleasure of breaking those gold-rimmed teeth appealed to Kinsolving in a savage way. It might not gain him anything—except needed emotional release—but he'd see.

He killed the repulsor field and let the vehicle slide along the ground on its underside. Fat blue sparks leaped into space as metal tore off and the car crashed into the side of the building. Kinsolving exploded from the interior in time to get his feet. Cameron came from inside, a curious expression on his face.

Kinsolving swung and connected with the man's

belly. Cameron doubled up, but the impact sent pain lancing all the way to Kinsolving's shoulder. It felt as if he'd struck a solid steel plate.

"Wh-what's wrong?" gasped Cameron.

"You turned me over to the Lorr."

"No, no! You've got it wrong! I was only doing as Mr. Humbolt wanted. Part of the escape. Send the Bizzies in the other direction so you can escape."

Kinsolving noticed that Cameron used the derogatory term for the aliens that Humbolt and Ala Markken had. He said, "Not a single shuttle is ready to launch. I talked with the technicians."

"They aren't in on this. Shuttle twenty-three's ready! Did you check it?" Cameron straightened. Kinsolving saw nothing in the man's face except for the glittering teeth and the cold, cold eyes.

"No," he admitted reluctantly.

"Then—damn! The Lorr! There they come. Quick. Hide inside. I'll try to decoy them away. Do it!"

Kinsolving obeyed the sharp command. He ducked inside and pressed himself against the inner wall, listening to what Cameron said to the alien police.

"Kinsolving. Where is he?" demanded the Lorr agent-captain. Kinsolving heard the shuffle of alien feet as four others joined Cameron. For a moment there was only silence, then a loud shriek of pain echoed across the still launch site.

Kinsolving hazarded a quick glance around the door. The agent-captain clutched his midsection, in-humanly bright crimson blood spurting around his snakelike fingers. His mouth worked to form another scream but death came first. He fell face forward onto the ground.

"There he is!" cried Cameron, pointing. "He shot your captain!"

Kinsolving got a quick glimpse of Cameron slipping a small tube into his coveralls. Then the door-

way filled with angry Lorr out to avenge the death
of their leader.

Kinsolving struck out, fist hitting the first Lorr
directly in the mouth. The alien stumbled back,
momentarily blocking the entrance. Kinsolving
reeled away, unsteady on his feet. He recovered
enough to dive through a window, plastic cutting at
his body as he went through. He landed heavily. For
an instant Kinsolving wondered why he had trouble
standing. The ground seemed unnaturally slippery.

He saw a small puddle of blood from his own cuts
had formed under his feet. He rolled to the side and
got up. Behind him the Lorr shouted for him to halt.

The world changed around Kinsolving. Time
dragged. He turned to see Cameron standing to one
side, an evil smile on his lips. Lorr comically tumbled from the building. The dead agent-captain lay
on the ground, muscle contractions shaking him.

Kinsolving felt as if he pushed through water to
get to the Lorr vehicle. He dropped into the uncomfortable seat and slapped the throttle forward. The
Lorr scattered as the car rocketed past them.

Without a vehicle to pursue him, the Lorr were
temporarily stranded. But Barton Kinsolving realized the reprieve would be brief.

He had nowhere to go, no one to turn to.

CHAPTER TEN

BARTON KINSOLVING found it more difficult to control the Lorr vehicle than he'd thought. The controls didn't respond properly and the seat was uncomfortable; it hadn't been designed for a bulky human. Weaving and wobbling from side to side, Kinsolving decided that he had to abandon the vehicle. The Lorr might have a tracing device inside. He had no idea how the Lorr police might think. Did it ever occur to them that someone might steal their vehicle?

He doubted it.

Pulling to the side of the road, Kinsolving got out and stretched his cramped limbs. He looked around and knew that it would be minutes before they found him. But he wouldn't surrender easily. He couldn't. Cameron had murdered the agent-captain and placed the blame all too firmly on Kinsolving. If Ala Markken received forty years in a primitive cell for ore theft and tax evasion. Kinsolving didn't want to think what the punishment would be for slaying a Lorr officer.

Forty years of torture? Kinsolving shuddered at the idea. Earth might have problems competing with the stargoing cultures and seem barbaric in comparison, but criminals were treated humanely.

Humanly, Kinsolving mentally corrected. The Lorr had their own ideas of punishment, and they didn't seem to include rehabilitation. Did they execute those convicted of capital offenses? He had no idea, nor did he want to find out.

Barton Kinsolving started hiking. On foot he had little chance against flyers and the repulsor-powered ground vehicles, but he might get lucky. How he had no idea.

But he had to try.

"This is a sorry chapter in human–Lorr history, Agent-General. I assure you that Interstellar Materials is not responsible, that we will do all within our power to capture this dangerous renegade." Kenneth Humbolt studied the Lorr officer to see if his lie had been accepted. It had.

"We do not understand how such a heinous crime could be committed," the Lorr said. "We do not slay each other. From all evidence, including the witness of your mechanic, this Kinsolving took a small explosive pellet weapon and fired it into the belly of the agent-captain."

Cameron nodded slowly, as if remembering a painful event in his life. "It was a silver tube, not twenty centimeters long. I heard a sound behind me, saw Supervisor Kinsolving in the doorway with it in his hand—and then he fired! There was only a small noise, then your officer doubled over holding his stomach." Cameron smirked in spite of the sour look that Humbolt shot him.

"What can we do to aid your search for him?" Humbolt asked.

"You need do nothing. My surveillance teams hunt him now. They will find him."

Humbolt shifted nervously from one foot to the other. "Uh, Agent-General, it's been several hours since you found the vehicle Kinsolving stole. Is there any progress in *capturing* him?"

"We are not used to conducting such hunts. None in my command can remember one; I contacted my superior. She cannot remember such a search, either."

"I again offer the full Interstellar Materials equipment and personnel for your official use, Agent-General. My mechanic is skilled in many areas. Perhaps he could construct a robot able to find Kinsolving's trail."

"Yes," cut in Cameron, suddenly eager for the hunt. "I know of certain ways that ordinary robot maintenance machines can be converted to efficient hunters."

"How is this possible?" the Lorr asked, face contorting in thought.

"Certain devices. Infrared scanners to follow heat imprints, footprints on the ground."

"This Kinsolving is hours gone."

"My sensors are capable of detecting a trail hours old." Cameron almost lost his temper. Humbolt motioned him to silence. The assassin paid him no heed. "There are other devices. Scent detectors. The slightest pheromone profile is traceable, after days or even weeks. I've found men in the midst of huge cities."

"For what reason?" asked the Agent-General. "Are you a policeman for Interstellar Materials?"

"Uh, no, nothing of that sort. This is . . . a hobby."

"I do not understand the word." The Lorr turned to an assistant, who worked feverishly at a translation computer. He showed the screen to his superior, who shook his head like a bird pecking at a worm. "There is no analog in our language for this 'hobby.'"

"That's not important," Humbolt cut in. "Please let us try to find Kinsolving for you."

"You do not seek this one of your own kind to aid in off-planet escape?" The Lorr seemed perplexed at this turn.

"Agent-General, my most fervent hope is that he

is brought to justice." Humbolt waited until the alien bobbed his head once more in agreement.

"Do what you will, but two of my officers will accompany your Cameron on the search."

"We wouldn't have it any other way," said Humbolt. For the first time, relief flooded throughout his body and allowed him to relax. When the alien left, Humbolt spun and faced Cameron.

"You fool! Don't be so damned eager. And try not to give away technology to them. They don't seem to have the IR detectors or SAWS for their robots."

"I know that part of the Plan," Cameron said. "There is no need to lecture me, Director."

"The Plan," mused Humbolt. "The damned Plan. You know that Markken spoke of it to Kinsolving?"

Cameron's eyebrows rose. "I had no idea. I would have burned him instead of the Bizzie if I'd known."

"She had no reason for mentioning it. He made her angry and it slipped out. She will have to be disciplined for that, but it won't be anything severe. Markken and the others will be rotated back to GT 4 when this matter with Kinsolving is settled."

"Could I be the one to discipline her?" asked Cameron. "She..."

"No!" Humbolt snapped. "She will play a larger role in the future. Markken has done well here. She's kept the Bizzies from bleeding us to death with their severance taxes, and the samarium from her thefts insures us of millions of brain-burners." Humbolt smiled crookedly. "She thinks the rare earths will be used only for a full fleet of starships otherwise denied us. She may yet learn the true use for the rare earths. Markken will do well for IM and the Plan in the future."

"And perhaps an ambitious director of Interstellar Materials has personal plans for her?" Cameron suggested.

"That is none of your concern. Get your robots out

and find that son of a bitch before the Bizzies do. I don't want him telling them anything he might have guessed about the Plan."

Cameron waved off the suggestion of ruin. "He is discredited in their amber eyes. Nothing your former supervisor has to say will be believed." Cameron's laugh echoed throughout the building.

"I hope so—for your sake." With that, Kenneth Humbolt stalked out. Cameron's mocking laugh followed him as he left.

Kinsolving couldn't believe his luck. He had hardly abandoned the Lorr vehicle when a heavily laden truck came along the road. As the repulsor field under the truck strained to hold the vehicle upright and propel its mass up the steep hill, Kinsolving raced out from his cover by the road and jumped onto the back. He almost lost his grip when the truck topped the hill and sped downward.

A quick twist and Kinsolving got into the back. The stench made him want to vomit, but he held down his rising gorge. He'd stowed away on a garbage truck from the city. Trying to decide where it was headed, Kinsolving rested and collected his wits. Events had moved too swiftly to do anything but react.

It was now time to reflect.

"Humbolt and IM want me dead—or in Lorr prison," he said. "Why? To cover up Ala's thefts?" He couldn't believe that. Kinsolving didn't delude himself for an instant. For the huge corporation his skills were more valuable than Ala's or any of the others'.

Or were they? The woman had mentioned a mysterious plan. The Plan, she had said. Kinsolving had heard the capital letters as she spoke. Interstellar Materials had to be involved; Kenneth Humbolt knew the details. They cheated the Lorr out of taxes, and Ala had mentioned that IM was responsible. Did IM have a secret construction project to build starships that the aliens knew nothing about?

"A war fleet?" Kinsolving mused. The idea of interstellar war had been one hotly debated when he'd been in college. The logistics presented problems no race could overcome. The distances were too great, the physics of the stardrive too cumbersome to move enough troops and materiel—and why lay waste to an entire planet? Wars were not simply killing your enemy. Something had to be gained.

Could Ala and Humbolt and the others at IM be so hostile toward all aliens that they'd consider planetary bombardment and genocide? Kinsolving found that difficult to believe. Stargoing races weren't clustered on single planets. To destroy all aliens would require resources far exceeding anything Earth could hope to muster.

Kinsolving snorted in disgust. Earth barely fed its own people. Jobs were scarce and many scholars pointed to this century as a new Dark Ages. This wasn't the time to raise the banner for a new crusade against aliens.

Or was it?

He rose and peered out the rear of the truck when it began to slow. Kinsolving didn't hesitate. He jumped and rolled to the side of the road rather than wait for eventual discovery. Rising up, he looked around. The truck had come to the Lorr sanitary torch where debris was fed into a plasma jet. The resulting increase in heat helped power the unit, making it partially self-sustaining.

"Garbage. I almost ended up as garbage."

He made his way across the gently rolling hills, taking a few minutes' break every hour to rest. Kinsolving had no idea where he went. Just getting away from the Lorr topped the list of priorities.

After he had found a secure hideout, he could worry about IM and Humbolt and the rest of the puzzle.

Standing atop a low hill, he looked toward the sunset. Dust had risen earlier in the day as a brisk wind came up, making the sunset gorgeous. He remembered the days he and Ala had watched the sunsets. A lump rose in his throat.

Those days were gone.

Kinsolving had no hint that anyone was closer than a hundred kilometers to him when a slight scraping sound caused him to turn. He then heard the hum from the robot as its repulsor field drove it up the hillside and bowled him over. He fought but the robot body had been electrified. The lightest touch made him wince. The robot powered down atop him. The shock he received stunned him.

Through a haze he saw Cameron and two Lorr standing over him. Cameron laughed and laughed and laughed.

Barton Kinsolving passed out.

"There is no honor in this sentence," the agent-general intoned. "Usual court procedure is for three officers to sit in final judgment." Kinsolving noted that seven were on the court. That made the matter even more serious.

He looked around the small room. Ala Markken sat with her hands folded in her lap, eyes straight ahead. He tried to catch her gaze and failed. On either side of her sat Cameron and Kenneth Humbolt. Both men looked satisfied with themselves.

Kinsolving wished he could free himself of the bonds holding him to the floor long enough to strangle both men. His mind turned over different ways of killing them, of which to kill first. He couldn't decide who would die first. Humbolt had betrayed him. The plot to fake the murder and turn the Lorr on his trail reeked of Humbolt's political manipulations. But Cameron had actually slain the Lorr officer. The expression of sheer delight on the man's face had told Kinsolving that Cameron was a psychopathic killer, the likes of which he had only heard of roaming about in the worst sections of Earth cities.

"We have reached a unanimous decision," the agent-general said. "Normal crimes are punishable by local imprisonment. This is no ordinary crime." The Lorr shivered delicately. "You are sentenced to life imprisonment on the world with no name."

Kinsolving frowned. He had no idea what this meant. Looking over his shoulder, he saw that Humbolt rose from his seat to protest. Cameron reached across and tugged on the director's sleeve and whispered for several seconds.

Kinsolving had no idea what they discussed, but it had to be the severity of his sentence. Humbolt had wanted the death penalty to remove all problems posed by Kinsolving's existence. But Cameron had convinced him that this sentence was as good.

Kinsolving shuddered at the idea of imprisonment worse than that the Lorr used on Ala Markken and the others.

"Agent-General," he spoke up. "What is the world with no name?"

The Lorr made a hand-whipping gesture. When he spoke it was to Humbolt and not to Kinsolving. "The world with no name is a planet used by many starfaring races. Only a select few know its location. Exile to this world is permanent. Starships land prisoners. No one ever leaves the world. Ever."

Kinsolving had never heard of such a planet. He tried to protest but Lorr guards unfastened the chains binding him to the floor and dragged him out of the room. For a brief instant, his eyes locked with Ala's.

Tears welled and ran down her cheeks. Other than this, she betrayed no emotion.

In shock, Kinsolving allowed his captors to shove him into a vehicle. In twenty minutes he was on a Lorr shuttle lifting for orbit. In forty, the starship shifted for the world with no name.

CHAPTER ELEVEN

BARTON KINSOLVING allowed the Lorr to do with him as they desired. The shock he felt at the repeated betrayals robbed him of all will until the alien starship shifted into orbit around the planet they refused to name.

Kinsolving experienced the gut-wrenching hyperspace transition and struggled to keep from vomiting. With his hands securely chained and another loop of chain around his waist fastened to a deck plate he wasn't able to move easily.

"Please," he called weakly from between chapped lips. The Lorr hadn't fed him or given him a drop of water since the sentence had been passed on Deepdig. Kinsolving tried to guess how long ago that had been and could only estimate four days. "Where are we?"

"Your home," snapped his guard. The alien sat in a comfortable couch and stared suspiciously at him, as if he'd get up and run away. Even if he could manage such a feat, as weak and battered emotionally as he was, Kinsolving had nowhere to go.

Interstellar Materials was no longer his employer. Kenneth Humbolt had betrayed him. His lover Ala Markken had forsaken him. The mysterious, murderous Cameron had made it seem that he'd committed a crime that had resulted in his exile. Kinsolving had nowhere to turn.

"What is it? Where is it?"

"The planet with no name," the guard said. "Only a few know its location. We use it for our . . . debris."

Kinsolving started to protest his innocence, then stopped. It would do no good. Even if the guard believed him—and there was no reason that he would—Kinsolving gained nothing. Every beat of his heart took a little more strength. He slumped back to the cold metal deck plate and curled up in the fetal position he had assumed throughout the four-day trip.

Four days. The alien starships were more efficient than those built on Earth. Somehow they escaped what, for Earth scientists, were "speed limits" in hyperspace, much as the speed of light limited travel in four-space. Kinsolving tried to decide if they'd come a hundred light years or a thousand from Deepdig.

In the end he came to the sorry conclusion that it no longer mattered. He believed the guard when he said that the location of the prison planet was a secret. And who would want to rescue Barton Kinsolving? Everything was tied up in such a neat, presentable package with him rotting on some forsaken planet tucked away at the edge of the universe.

Interstellar Materials maintained its rare earth mines on Deepdig. Ala and the others were cleared of the felony charges. And the Lorr believed they had brought the guilty party to justice, not only for killing an agent-captain but also for the heinous crime of tax evasion and stealing oxide ores.

And it was all part of what Ala Markken had called the Plan. Like the prison planet below the orbiting starship, this, too, was a secret, a mystery, something Kinsolving would never discover before he died.

"Out," came the guard's rough command. Tentaclelike fingers circled Kinsolving's wrists and pulled him erect. Try as he might, Kinsolving couldn't get his muscles to obey. He sank back to the deck. Resolve not to show weakness in the face of such adversity made him stand on shaking legs. This time he did not collapse. The guard shoved him roughly through a passageway to a shuttle. When Kinsolving could no longer walk, the guard grabbed the chains and dragged him.

By the time the shuttle touched down on the planet's surface, Kinsolving was more dead than alive.

"Your new home. May you live long and suffer horribly." The guard heaved Kinsolving out the small hatchway and slammed it behind immediately. The man pulled himself up to a sitting position. The world swung in crazy circles around him. He heard fuel pumps working to feed the ignition chambers in the tiny shuttle.

It came to him through the thick mist of confusion and abuse that he would be fried unless he avoided the shuttle's rocket blast. No laser powered this ship into orbit. There wasn't even a formal landing field. Some grass had been scorched off a patch of dirt in the prairie. This appeared to be the only hint that anyone existed—or had ever existed —on the face of the planet.

Kinsolving struggled to drag himself away from the shuttle. The hot exhaust gases scorched his back and set tiny fires burning in his clothing when the shuttle launched. Rolling over and over put out the fires and left Kinsolving staring up at a heavily overcast sky. The leaden clouds billowed and gathered directly above. The rains, when they came, brought Kinsolving much needed water and the surcease of unconsciousness.

* * *

"You're looking better," came the voice speaking in a guttural mangling of Interspace, the lingua franca used by a score of spacefaring races. Kinsolving tried to blink and experienced a surge of panic. "Calm, now, calm. You're not blind. Here." A rag was taken from Kinsolving's eyes. He squinted at the tiny fire blazing merrily. He reached up to rub his temples. For a moment, he worried that something was wrong.

"My chains. They're gone!" Kinsolving repeated it in Interspace, when his first words produced no response.

"Of course they are. There's no need of your going around with them, now is there? Unless you want them back? But that's not possible. Sold them. Metal's scarce."

"You sold them?" Although weak, Kinsolving felt better than he had since leaving Deepdig. He sat up and turned to face his benefactor. Kinsolving almost yelped in surprise. The creature sitting across the fire from him could hardly be described as human or even humanoid.

"Got a fair price. Wanted to split it with you, we did, but you owed, so we took your part. Only fair, only fair."

Kinsolving rubbed his wrists and reveled in the freedom he'd thought he would never again experience. And the hollowness in his belly seemed filled.

"You fed me?"

"That we did," the toadlike creature said. Long, powerful hind legs moved it around and tiny hands more human than those of the Lorr worked at a dish and spoon carved from wood. The food in the bowl vanished into a huge mouth lined with dual rows of sharp, wicked teeth. The forward-looking eyes and those needlelike teeth told Kinsolving that

his rescuer was a predator and a carnivore by evo-
lution.

"Thanks."

"Nothing on this world's free," the creature said.
The sharp eyes fixed on Kinsolving and bored into
his soul. "You don't think a few links of chain are
enough repayment, do you?"

"Perhaps, perhaps not. I need to know something."

"Information's costly. Know things and you can do
things."

"You can't eat information," said Kinsolving.
"When they put me here—"

"Who is this 'they'?" asked the creature. It bobbed
up and down on its strong hind legs. Kinsolving
tried not to think of frog legs. His stomach rumbled
at the thought of Earth food.

"The Lorr. Aren't they the ones who sent you
here, too?"

"Don't know any Lorr. Might have heard of them
but forgot. Too many damn races out there with
their fancy laws and ways. The Rua'Kinth convicted me and sent me here. May their legs turn
weak!"

"I'm Barton Kinsolving."

"Never heard of that race, either," the creature
said. Kinsolving explained that this was his name,
a concept the creature had obviously encountered
before but hadn't successfully mastered.

"Can't understand why individual names are
needed," the creature said. "We come from Sus-
sonssa. Great hunting, good people. No rules like
out there." A tiny hand pointed upward.

"Is it always overcast?" asked Kinsolving, trying
to find a wink of starlight and failing.

"Always. Never seen clear skies once in more

than a year on-planet. No one else has, either. One reason they chose it, maybe."

"What are we supposed to do? Report to a jailer?"

The creature laughed heartily at this—at least Kinsolving hoped the strange croaking noises were laughter.

"We go and come as we please. Eat, live, not eat, die. It matters nothing to them. We are free to roam the planet for the rest of our lives."

Kinsolving turned cold inside. He had harbored some faint hope of reprieve, of bribing a guard, of escape. Now it evaporated like mist in a sun he would never see. The Lorr and the other alien races simply dropped their prisoners onto this planet and let them survive or not. If only a handful of navigators knew the location of the world, rescue attempts would be impossible.

There were too many stars to search simply to find one planet. And Kinsolving knew of no one interested in finding him. He was written off, a null, a closed chapter in IM history.

"Then there aren't any laws?" asked Kinsolving.

"Only what we make. Criminals are not good at enforcing laws. If you do not like the local laws, move. The planet is wide and big. Travel is by foot, but you have plenty of time. All the time left in your life!" Again the creature laughed.

"You seem cheerful about it. Why?"

"You laugh or you cry. We laugh."

Kinsolving glanced around. As far as he could tell, they were alone. "Why do you refer to yourself in the plural?"

"Sussonssans are telepathic. Hard to be alone. Only fourteen of us on this world, but from time to time we join physically in harmony and community."

"Is there any chance you could communicate and

when the next ship lands bringing—" The creature's harsh laughter cut off Kinsolving's words.

"Not possible. Not. Always they scan the ground with sensors before landing. And the landings might happen one-two-three soon or be years apart. And they land in different places. And—"

"I get the picture," said Kinsolving, feeling glum. "How do you live?"

"Poorly, but we live."

"What do you do? Farm?"

"Hunter gatherer is all we can do. No metal, no hope of making more. Light metal planet, this one is. Your chains are valuable for what they can be made into. Why develop city? Most of us are thieves and we would only steal from each other." This struck the creature as hilarious. Tiny hands held bulging mottled gray sides as it laughed.

For the first time, Kinsolving had the sense of true desolation fall like a cloak around him. What crime had his benefactor committed? Murder? Worse? What would be worthy of lifelong exile? Tax evasion? Kinsolving didn't think that was likely.

"So we just survive as long as we can, then we die?" he asked.

"Is that not the definition of life?"

"I expect more."

"What a strange race yours is. You resemble several we have seen, but you are much uglier and stupider."

"The feeling's mutual."

The creature made a choking noise, then hopped around to hunker down beside Kinsolving by the fire. "We can do well as a team, you and we. My brains and your height will go far on this world."

"How?"

"The beast to whom we sold the chains. He has many links garnered over the years. He sharpens them and mounts them as spear heads. Some knives. We can steal these from him."

"Is this the only way to live?" asked Kinsolving.

"Why live any other? To scrabble for roots in this desolate place is difficult. The grains growing wild are poor fodder. What is not dusty and flat on this world is rocky and mountainous."

"Oceans?"

"Who knows or cares?" Before the creature could utter another word, the sound of movement brought them both around.

Kinsolving shrieked and rolled onto his back, feet going out. He caught a humanoid creature in the belly. A hand with a knife slashed for his throat; Kinsolving snared the wrist and pulled, using the humanoid's momentum to pull it on over and land it in the fire.

The creature screeched and tried to escape the flames. The Sussonssan's tiny hands pinned it where it lay until its clothing caught fire. Only then did Kinsolving's benefactor allow the creature to escape. It fled into the night, a living torch lighting a small dirt path.

"We were careless, but your reflexes are good. Now, about the one with the metal."

"Wait," said Kinsolving, confused. "Who was that? *What* was it?"

"That?" The Sussonssan waved its tiny hands about in a gesture of dismissal. "A predator. But we are all predators here. It thought to find an easy meal, a new cloak, a weapon."

"A weapon!" The Sussonssan pounced on the ground near the fire and rooted through the dirt until it found the knife. Tiny fingers circling the hilt, it held up the weapon. "A knife! And a fine one. I will take this as payment for the blood debt you owe me."

"Done," said Kinsolving, not wanting any more to do with the ugly creature.

"Oh, we will make such a fine pair, you and we. Your ignorance will fade soon under our excellent tutelage. You will have nothing to fear and will prosper on this poor world. Wait to see if we do not speak the truth!"

Barton Kinsolving worried that the Sussonssan might be right. He couldn't simply give up and die. But what manner of life could he lead, preying on the other convicts, having them prey on him? That wasn't a fit life.

It wasn't a fit life, but it was one he'd have to lead. Kinsolving settled down to listen to his mentor expound on how they would approach this new crime and the rewards to be reaped.

CHAPTER TWELVE

BARTON KINSOLVING did not fit into the ways of
the prison planet. Life proved a cheap commodity
when no one had anything more to look forward to
than a lifetime of wandering the barren planet's
face. But Kinsolving refused to kill for sport, unlike
his Sussonssan companion. The toadlike being
thrilled to murder, whether it was dropping a heavy
rock on another's head or running him down and
using those powerful hind legs to pummel him to
death.

"You lack the proper attitude, Kinsolving," the
toad creature told him one day after they had been
together for almost two planetary months. Kinsolving had learned what he could do and wouldn't do,
and had managed to survive. But as much as the
Sussonssan called them a team, Kinsolving knew
that it wasn't true.

If the toad being needed something Kinsolving
had and the human refused to hand it over, those
powerful hind legs would kick out and the sharp
talons on the toes would slice open Kinsolving's
belly. And the Sussonssan would feel not one whit of
remorse.

Kinsolving knew why the creatures had been
placed on this world even though he had never
asked. Without any hint of conscience, the being
would prove too much a menace for any civilized
society. The only question that burned inside Kin-

solving, and the one he didn't dare ask, concerned the other aliens. If this Sussonssan maintained telepathic contact, were the others also as lacking in conscience? And what of their entire race?

The prisoners Kinsolving encountered in his wanderings tended to be of similar bent. It almost brought him to tears thinking that the Lorr considered him a worthy addition to this planet's prison population.

"There are ways of getting what you want without killing," Kinsolving told the toad creature. "I'm not above thievery to get what we need. I may not like it, but I'll do it."

He snorted and shivered a little in the cold. Theft had kept him alive for the first month. He had desperately needed clothing against the frigid nights. Without money or anything to trade, theft had been his only recourse. Occasional lean-tos constituted cities on this planet, and no one trusted another enough to "hire" help. Mostly, the prisoners lived nomadic existences, drifting from one place to another, any spot the equal of the last—or the next.

"But we kill for pleasure. Do you not get a thrill feeling your enemy dying on your talons?" The Sussonssan canted its head to one side and peered at Kinsolving. "Your talons *are* feeble weapons. Perhaps this explains your lack of enjoyment."

"On my planet argument takes the place of killing."

"How dull."

"Not really," said Kinsolving. "If you beat an opponent in an argument, you're likely to be able to do it again. We can win repeatedly. You can only kill an opponent once."

"True," mused the toad creature. "But your kind tends to confuse quantity and quality. It must be a wan reward to duel with words. A thousand victories cannot equal one rimmed with blood."

"Are all your people like you?"

"All on this planet," the Sussonssan answered without hesitation.

Kinsolving let the matter drop. They were engaged in trying to survive—again. The toad being had convinced him that they both needed knives before making the trek across the dusty plains and to the foothills of mountains Kinsolving saw struggling up into the cloud layer. Kinsolving hoped to scale those peaks, get above the omnipresent clouds and glimpse the stars. He had no reason to think he could figure out the planet's location, but he had to try.

Kinsolving had to admit that seeing the night's star field might not even help. He was no navigator or astronomer. The constellation might be entirely twisted from those he had grown up with as a youth on Earth. There had been few visible, thanks to the light pollution from the cities, but he had studied books. When he had been stationed on Deepdig he often lay alone outside his house to simply gaze at the stars. Those patterns had been slightly altered from the ones he'd learned, but not much. Deepdig was only a hundred light years from home.

But this prison world? Kinsolving had no way of knowing if what he'd see would mean anything to him. Trying, however, gave some imitation of purpose to his existence.

"This one's weapons make for good use," the Sussonssan said in its guttural tone. "See the knife on display? Such a fine working of a chain link into a double-edged blade."

"On display? You mean stuck in his belt?"

"Same thing."

Kinsolving had to admit that their intended victim did fine work. A humanoid lacking hair and a nose, the greenish-skinned being went about his work with an air of indifference that Kinsolving had

come to associate with all those who had been on-
planet longer than a few years. What mattered
when escape was impossible, when even striking
out at your captors proved beyond your abilities?

Kinsolving had been on this world only two
months and this lethargy threatened to possess
him.

"Now. We go. You wait and watch. There is much
we do not like about this theft," the Sussonssan
said.

"What? I don't see anything wrong." Kinsolving
spoke to thin air. The toad creature hopped away,
tiny hands waving in the air. The humanoid looked
up, his tiny eyes showing no true intelligence; the
Sussonssan struck. Heavily muscled legs powered
its talons forward to rip and rake.

But the toad being had been right in its caution.
The humanoid moved with a speed that belied its
bulky frame. The taloned foot missed its target by
centimeters. By the time the Sussonssan had recovered for another attack, the humanoid had drawn
the knife they coveted and held it in a three-fin-
gered, huge-thumbed hand. The humanoid's muscles bulged and he began sucking in noisy gusts of
air, as if he had already run a long race. The hair-
less dome of the humanoid's head began to sprout
thick, throbbing veins as the greenish pallor vanished and was replaced by a bright pink as the oxygen level required for fighting rose within the
humanoid's body.

Kinsolving hesitated, then launched into the attack. Between the two of them, they could steal the
humanoid's knife no matter how strong or agile the
pinkly glowing being proved. Kinsolving didn't like
this but resources were scarce. Without a weapon
on the journey to the mountains, Kinsolving wasn't
sure he could make it. The toad creature had shown
him several small predators that abounded on the

plains. Without more than a sharpened stick, Kinsolving had no chance against their ripping fangs.

He came in low, thinking to tackle the humanoid. Inhuman joints thwarted him. Kinsolving grabbed and found the humanoid lifting one foot and rotating ninety degrees on the planted leg. Like the Lorr, this humanoid had enhanced mobility because of differently hinged knees. Kinsolving rolled free and stared. He couldn't tell for certain, but it seemed that the alien had a universal joint instead of a more human knee. The humanoid swung about, knife flashing in search of a berth in Kinsolving's back. Only the Sussonssan's quicker reflexes saved Kinsolving. The powerful toad leg swept out and countered the slash.

Blood spurted and momentarily blinded Kinsolving. He hastily wiped it from his eyes, worrying that it was his own. It wasn't. By the time his vision cleared, he saw two bodies on the ground. The man dropped to examine the toad creature.

The humanoid's knife had severed a throat artery, killing almost instantly. But one taloned foot had raked along the humanoid's leg and up into the belly. Kinsolving thought a renal artery had been cut. He held down his rising gorge at the sight of so much blood. A shaky hand picked up the fallen knife.

Two lives had been snuffed out for this.

"The stars had better be there," he said softly. "Dammit, they'd better be!"

Crude knife clutched in his hand, Kinsolving rose and stared at the two corpses. The Sussonssan's fellow beings would know of its death; telepathic contact might be traumatic, but they knew. Kinsolving looked around for a soft spot in the ground to dig two graves and found only thin, rocky soil. The sound of approaching animals convinced him that doing what he considered a decent thing wasn't possible. The scavengers on this world were savage. A single man with only a knife stood little chance against a hungry pack.

Kinsolving abandoned the two to the pack of roving carrion eaters and ran as if his life depended on it—and it did. Seldom did the scavenger pack find enough to eat; they weren't above stalking prey and worrying it to death.

Into the night Kinsolving ran until exhaustion overcame him. He found a rough-barked tree and crawled onto the lower limbs, finding the vertex of two branches where he could lean back and try to relax. The Sussonssan had chided him often about his affinity for trees. The toad creature had claimed it came from racial memory, that only inferior beasts evolved from the arboreal. Truly superior ones, such as itself, rose from the primordial slime.

"Is it better to be a fallen angel or a devil risen from the muck?" Kinsolving mused. Was there any difference if both ended up in the same place, enduring the same conditions? He had no answer for this or any other problem plaguing him. The distant sound of the noisily dining scavenger pack in his ears, he eventually fell into a light, troubled sleep.

Barton Kinsolving kept away from other prisoners during the next month as he hiked toward the mountain range. The Sussonssan hadn't been a friend, but it had been someone to talk with, to keep from going crazy with loneliness and frustration. The passage of time helped Kinsolving come to grips with the isolation. He even came to prefer it. The others on this world were deadly criminals, locked away here and forgotten so that they would be unable to perpetrate future crimes on their societies. Kinsolving had given up hoping to find others like himself, others wrongly accused and sentenced. Trusting no one else—daring to trust no one else—had its drawbacks, but it also had benefits.

The meager food he gleaned from the soil kept him alive, adequately if not well. For two it would have been starvation or worse. Always sleeping with one eye open to trouble from a travelling companion didn't appeal to him.

Kinsolving stopped and cocked his head to one side, listening. The scavenger packs he had to avoid. He wasn't strong or quick enough to fight them. The smaller predators he might deal with using the stolen knife that had cost the toad creature his life.

"Meat," he said aloud, his mouth watering at the thought. "The predators taste like shit but are better than nothing." He had found little except for tubers to be roasted and swallowed as quickly as possible. But meat? Was that the meaning of the sound he heard?

Kinsolving dropped to his knee and allowed the high grass to partially hide him. Slowly scanning a full three-hundred-sixty degrees, he frowned. The sound grew louder, and he couldn't identify it. When it rose to a shrill whine, he clamped hands over ears in a vain attempt to block it out.

Seconds after Kinsolving thought the sound would kill him, he saw the lead gray clouds part and a starship come through, standing upright on its emergency rockets. Whoever was inside had to have incredible trouble to land a spacegoing vessel on a planet. Kinsolving knew that the emergency rockets were intended for a simple sit-down and nothing more. Any repairs that needed doing would have to be to the main engines or the ship would be permanently grounded.

Then the lethargy that had fallen on him evaporated and the fact hit him that escape lay at hand.

Even before the rockets had cut off and the high-pitched whine had died, Kinsolving was up and running for the ship. He recognized the lines, even from a kilometer away. He ran toward the most modern and powerful Earth-built speedster available for private use. Why they had landed on the prison world didn't matter to him. That they had and were probably human did.

He could talk his way off this world! And if that failed, Kinsolving's strong fingers brushed lightly over the knife slid through his belt. That knife had been responsible for two intelligent beings' deaths. Another wouldn't matter.

Not if it meant his freedom!

He reached the scorched area around the ship's base and slowed, cautiously picking his way through burning clumps of grass. A smooth whirring noise drew his attention upward to the emergency hatch. Someone stood there, waving to him.

"Hello!" he called. "Can you lower a line to let me into the ship?"

"There are natives!" came a delightful squeal. "I don't even know where I crashed. Oh, this is wonderful!"

"A line," he pleaded. "Or do you have a small elevator?"

"You seem very human. I didn't think there'd be many aliens who looked exactly like me." A giggle. "Well, you're not *exactly* like me. You're a man."

Kinsolving walked back a few paces and peered up at the hatch, squinting into the sunlight reflecting off the highly polished silver hull. "I'm from Earth."

"What a coincidence. So am I," came the voice. For the first time, Kinsolving saw more than the waving hand. A woman leaned far out and peered down at him. He frowned. The distance obscured her features but something appeared wrong. The

general shape was right, but the details seemed...
different. Kinsolving hadn't been away from human
society long enough to forget what a woman looked
like.

But it didn't matter to him if this one had a
highly contagious case of Buck-Babb's sarcoma. She
was human; she was a way off this prison world.

"I need to get into your ship!" he called again.
"Please!"

"Can you fix shift engines?" she yelled. "The main
drive went out. I have no idea how to even begin
fixing them."

"Yes, yes, I know how," Kinsolving lied. His hopes
for escape began to fade. Before he could fix the engines, the alien keepers in orbit would have homed
in on the grounded ship. Would they lob an atomic
and convert the entire area into radiant energy or
would they simply laser the ship to insure that it
didn't lift again?

Kinsolving had passed the point of mere survival.
If he couldn't escape, he'd prefer total destruction.

"Here's a line. Can you use it?" A slender loading
crane poked out from the hatch, a line attached. It
lowered—too slowly for Kinsolving's liking. But it
finally reached him. He tied a double bowline in the
end and slipped his arms through. He motioned to
the woman to get him back to the ship's hatch.

The trip up the side of the speedster dragged on
for an eternity. Kinsolving rotated slowly in his
sling, getting first a look at the barren plains he
had crossed and then the ship's hull. He preferred
the stargoing ship to the prairie. One held hope, the
other only death and evil memories.

"Hello," the woman said when he reached the
hatch. She reached out a dainty hand and helped
him swing into the air lock. "My, aren't you the bar-
barian? Are you some primitive warrior stalking
his prey on this world?" She giggled.

Kinsolving stood and stared for a moment. The woman was beautiful, short blond hair intricately coiffured with platinum wire and pearls. But Kinsolving had seen more gorgeous women in his time; that wasn't the cause of his speechlessness. She smiled and her cheeks changed from a natural hue to a pastel green. A broader smile when she saw his reaction caused swirling colors to flow in a kaleidoscope over her face, turning her into something both alluring and frightening.

"Do you like the dye job? I got it done just before I left Earth."

"Dye job? I don't..."

"It's all the rage. The dyes are injected just below the skin. Oh, the needles hurt a teeny bit, but not much. As my mood changes, so does the color."

"And physical movement changes the pattern," Kinsolving guessed. The woman's pout altered both color and design.

"I wanted to tell you that, but you already knew."

"Sorry," Kinsolving said, confused. "I'm—" He paused for an instant. Should he lie or should he give his real name. Kinsolving decided that his infamy wouldn't have reached Earth. He had been totally forgotten by now. He gave his real name.

"Charmed," she said, curtsying. "And I'm Lark Versalles. This is my ship. Do you like it?" The blonde struck a pose so that she turned and showed her profile to him. What had at first seemed a chaste blouse for a woman so daring in her facial makeup now changed. The sunlight struck the material and turned parts transparent.

"Do you like it?" she asked. "A little something I found on one of those alien planets. At one of their strange market places. I had the cloth made into a blouse. I have no idea what *they* intended it for. But the effect is stunning, don't you agree?"

Her breasts appeared bare, then covered, then partially hidden. Kinsolving had to agree.

"You seem confused," Lark Versalles said. "Are you ill?"

"Ill?" Kinsolving fought to regain his wits. He had expected only a staid captain and interminable argument about leaving the planet. He hadn't believed anyone like Lark could exist starside of Earth's upper classes.

"Sick. Possessed of demons. I don't know. I can see if the medibot is working. I doubt it. Oh, nothing on this horrid ship works for me. Daddy bought it for me and said it was the latest in self-repairing and all that, but it just doesn't work."

"Work," Kinsolving said. His plight came rushing back. They had to lift—soon. If they didn't, he would be stranded forever on the prison world. "What went wrong? Stardrives don't break down."

"Well, Mr. Kinsolving, this one did." Lark smiled almost shyly and moved closer, her hand resting lightly on his arm. "May I call you Barton?"

"Of course. But—"

"I've never been this close to a criminal before. I mean, a dangerous one. Daddy is hardly what you'd call honest. And no one who works for him is, either. But they're not dangerous, unless you have a company they want. Then they can be vicious with mergers and sinking fund debentures and all that."

"How do you know I'm a convict?" he asked.

"Those dreadful aliens in orbit sent a warning. You *are* a criminal, aren't you?"

"They convicted me, but—"

She silenced him with her lips. Her lush body crushed against his. Kinsolving started to push her away and then stopped. When Lark broke off the kiss, her face flushed blues and greens.

"You are *dangerous*," she said breathlessly. "This is going to be fun!"

"The aliens in orbit. What did they tell you?"

"This is some sort of prison colony. A Botany Bay. You know Earth history, don't you? Of course you do. You're from Earth." Her hand roved over his chest, his belly, lower. "Oh, yes, you're human. Very, very human."

"Lark, please. They might try to keep us here, to stop us from leaving."

"They wouldn't dare! Daddy'd never permit it."

"The ship's engines. Show me what's wrong with them."

"Oh, you think those ugly things in orbit might try to *stop* us? This is going to be great fun!" She grabbed his grimy hand and led him through the ship's narrow corridors to a work panel near the sealed engine room. Lark pointed to a single large red warning light.

Kinsolving had no immediate idea what might have malfunctioned in the engine. He'd always heard that the precision machines functioned flawlessly—or blew up. Seldom did a starship manage to limp into drydock to be repaired. It just wasn't the nature of hyperspace flight to allow even minor accidents.

"Where's the computer console?" he asked. Kinsolving looked around, trying to find operating instructions.

"Computer? Oh, it must be here somewhere. They put them all over the ship. So confusing, don't you agree? Let me try this one." Lark toggled a switch on the bulkhead.

A high-pitched, stilted alien voice echoed over a speaker. "You will not leave this world. You will remain where you are or your vessel will be destroyed. Respond or we will consider you a renegade and open fire."

Kinsolving and Lark stared at each other, his dark eyes locking into her light blue ones.

"Do you think they really mean it?" she asked in a tiny voice.

An answer to her question came with stunning suddenness. The ship rocked from side to side on its hydraulic jacks as the aliens in orbit opened laser fire.

CHAPTER THIRTEEN

BARTON KINSOLVING hit the button to cycle shut all air locks. The searing impact of the plasma against the side of the ship rocked the speedster on its jacks.

"Why are they doing this?" Lark Versalles asked innocently. "I haven't done anything."

"Not yet, you haven't," Kinsolving said. "But you will."

"I will?" she said, almost happily. "This is becoming more photonic by the second. What am I going to do?"

"Help a convict escape." Kinsolving staggered and went to his knees. A laser blast raked the side of the ship. The gunners in orbit had found their range.

"They weren't lying," she said. "You *are* a criminal. How exciting!"

Sweat poured down Kinsolving's face. He looked over the control console for the hyperspace engines. He knew nothing about such mechanisms, but he was an engineer, a good one, and his life depended on fixing the engine and getting into space.

"What happened? When the engines died on you?"

"Nothing. I was just trying to get a message through to Dinky and—"

"A message?" Kinsolving demanded, cutting her off. "What do you mean?"

"I turned on the com-unit and powered up to contact Dinky. He's back on Earth—just getting ready to leave, actually—so I made sure the power level was at max."

"Didn't anyone ever tell you that you can't make radio contact through hyperspace? That it'll overload the engines?"

"Oh, I suppose they have," Lark said. The dyes under her cheeks turned a light pink, then suffused with pastel blues and greens. "Everyone's always telling me I can't do this and I can't do that. They're wrong, mostly."

"Not this time," Kinsolving said, hurrying now. Two more laser strikes rocked the ship. "There's infinite drain if you're in hyperspace and try to use the radio. I'm no physicist and don't know why. Usually there are cutoffs to protect the circuits. Here!"

He pulled off the panel covering and found a smaller board with a trio of toggle switches, all in the Off position. Kinsolving flipped them to On. Power hummed deep in the innards of the speedster's sealed stardrive engine.

"Why, you're a genius. You fixed it!"

"What did the guards in orbit tell you?"

"Oh, the usual warnings. Don't land, don't do this and that. They didn't say they'd fire on me. Not exactly."

Kinsolving rushed to the cockpit, Lark trailing behind and protesting that she didn't like being ignored. Kinsolving dropped into the comfortable acceleration couch and stared at the controls. Red lights danced, each showing an onboard failure from the laser barrage. But he had no trouble locating the launch sequencer. The elegant starship had been equipped with only the finest.

"Wait, don't!" cried Lark.

Kinsolving didn't hesitate. The timer gave less than five seconds before launch. Kinsolving found himself crushed in the couch, pinned by not only his own increased weight but also by Lark Versalles'. The woman had stumbled and fallen across him when the rockets ignited. Kinsolving struggled to pull her into the couch alongside. He managed to get her squarely on top of him.

The dye patterns writhing just under the woman's translucent skin turned paler and paler as the strain of launch acceleration mounted, but Lark managed to lift her head and peer down into Kinsolving's face.

"Never done this before. This is fun!"

Her mouth crushed hard against his, both passion and acceleration bruising his lips. Kinsolving struggled but Lark held the high ground and controlled him until the rockets died suddenly.

She cried out in surprise, floating up and off, weightless. "We're in orbit already! That was over too soon!"

"Not too soon," muttered Kinsolving. "Just in time." He worked his way across the control panel, seeing that the fuel for the emergency rockets had been fully expended. There wouldn't be any maneuvering using steering jets, not now. But he didn't intend docking or even staying in orbit long enough to need them.

"Intruder starship," blared the speaker. "You will cease all attempt to leave this planet. You will be destroyed instantly if you attempt escape."

"Do they mean it?" Lark asked, one slender leg curled around a stanchion. "They *did* fire at us with their lasers, though they weren't good shots."

"Good enough," said Kinsolving. "Several external sensors are blown out." His fingers worked faster now.

"What are you doing?" she cried. "You're preparing for star shift. You can't do that!"

"Why not?"

"But we don't have time to compute a destination. You're launching at random. And they did warn us."

"They can't have us in their sights or they'd have vaporized us instantly. That's a bluff. They have to fire their lasers directly through the planet's atmosphere," he said, checking relative locations of speedster and space station. "Too much beam attenuation to do real damage—for another few minutes."

"You'd just *go?*" Lark asked, amazed at the concept.

"What's wrong with that? You want excitement, don't you?"

"Oh, yes!"

"Then that's what I'll furnish. Lost among the stars. A random destination. Think of the romance in that."

"A friend of mine was lost for six years," Lark said, dubious of the adventure Kinsolving offered. The colors moving just below the surface of her skin began a slow dance from light, pastel shades to darker hues.

As he spoke, he worked at the controls. His eyes kept darting to the sensor picking up the signal from the orbiting space station. Another few seconds would bring the speedster back into range.

He slammed his hand down hard on the sequencer again. This time the shift into hyperspace occurred instantaneously. Kinsolving's stomach turned inside out and a kaleidoscope of colors danced before his eyes as the stardrive worked its mathematical magics on the curvature of fourspace.

The universe as he knew it vanished as light became too slow. His optic nerve refused to believe the lies this new universe told it. Kinsolving swayed dizzily, his ears roaring. A phantom song echoed through the din, more structured than electronic discharges from a gas giant planet but less ordered than true music.

Fingers tingling and his stomach tied into acid-filled knots, Kinsolving fought to regain control of his senses. He held on to the sides of the couch for several minutes until his senses quieted and he could sit up without an attack of dizziness. The distant music faded to nothingness and his eyes again believed the world around him. Only the churning of his gut remained.

"Lark?" he called. "Are you all right?" Kinsolving hadn't given the woman a chance to secure herself before the shift; there hadn't been any time left. The guard station had been preparing to turn this fine ship into molten aluminum and sublimated carbon.

"Fine. I'm fine," she said in a voice that betrayed that she wasn't.

Kinsolving swung out of the couch and paused for a moment to allow his legs to regain circulation. In the pseudogravity of hyperspace he could move about as easily as if he stood on the prison planet's surface—but he was free! He had escaped the planet from which no one had ever escaped before!

"Let me help you," he offered. His hands went under her slender arms. He heaved Lark to her feet. The swirling subcutaneous dyes provided the only color in her face—and he did not like the dark grays and ebonies intermixing. "Are you sure you're not hurt?" he repeated.

"Photonic!" she said. The woman's face began to glow with brighter greens and blues. When the decorative patterns turned crimson and silver he knew she meant what she said. "But I *loved* it in the acceleration couch." Her arms locked around him like steel bands. She kissed him deeply and long. Kinsolving found himself not only liking it but responding with all the fervor of a man lost to his own kind for long months.

"Um," he said, finally breaking off. "Nice, yes, but I've got to figure out where we're heading. It wouldn't do to get too lost."

"Moira was lost for six years, but she didn't have someone like you along to help pass the time." Lark's face radiated hot reds and purples that formed into tiny islands on her cheeks. Her arousal was obvious.

"Being lost isn't my intention," he said. "This is a fabulous speedster. Did your father buy it for you?" Kinsolving couldn't imagine the wealth that could purchase such an expensive ship for private use.

"Oh, not exactly. His company owns it, actually, but they give him anything he wants. And he gives me anything I want." She smiled and reached out, her fingers lightly caressing Kinsolving's cheek. "But that's boring. Where would you *want* to go?"

Kinsolving hadn't planned that far ahead. Only an hour earlier his plan had been to crawl up the side of a mountain, get above the ever present clouds and simply look at the nighttime sky to discover where the prison world might be in the cosmos. Escape hadn't been a part of his expectations, not after the first few weeks on the planet.

"Gamma Tertius 4, I suppose," he said. Kinsolving wondered if appealing to Chairman Fremont, explaining to the ancient man what had happened, would help. He had no idea. But something more than Interstellar Materials' headquarters lay on the desolate world. Kenneth Humbolt would be on GT 4. And perhaps Ala Markken would have been duty rotated there, also.

Ala! A void formed in Kinsolving's heart. How

much of his woe had come from the woman? Much?
Little? Had Humbolt lied to her, too, and caused her
to betray her lover? Was this part of the Plan she
had told him of when she'd been imprisoned by the
Lorr?

"Oh, tachyonic!" cried Lark. "I just *love* Gamma
Tertius 4. The parties there are the best anywhere.
IM knows how to make everyone feel so . . . good!"

"You've been to GT 4?" he asked.

"Many times. It's in the ship's nav-computer."
Lark frowned in thought. "But if we don't know
where we are now, that's not going to help, is it?"

"It might." Kinsolving wasn't adept at naviga-
tion. He knew so little beyond how to worry ore
from reluctant rock that it bothered him now. His
experiences had seemed broad until he had to face
harsh reality. The toad being on the prison world
had taught him more about survival than an upbringing on Earth had—and Kinsolving's childhood
hadn't been easy.

Kinsolving settled down and began working his
way slowly across the panel, making certain he
knew the function of every control. It proved easier
than programming a robominer. The starship's de-
signer hadn't wanted to force crew and passengers
into any hard work, either physical or mental.

"I have it," Kinsolving said, leaning back and
staring at the board. "We're going to have to drop
out to get a fix, but that shouldn't be too hard to
do."

"Do we have to do it right now? Those awful
guards might be following us." Lark pouted prettily.

Kinsolving considered. It wasn't likely that the
prison world guards had followed. Only routine
flights arrived and departed. Why try to trace the
hypertrail of a starship? Kinsolving knew it was
possible, but it required sophisticated equipment

not likely to be in the guards' arsenal. They orbited the planet and did little. Their poor work with the laser proved that, although Kinsolving knew that he'd been very, very lucky. Beam attenuation had robbed the laser of much of its destructive power.

And he had launched the speedster before the atmospheric shield could be pulled away by the space station's orbit.

"They won't track us," he said.

"Are you *really* a criminal?" Lark Versalles asked. Her eyes seemed to grow larger and shift colors. Kinsolving blinked, wondering if this were a trick of light or if the woman had surgically altered her eyes, too. Since she wore her expensive finery just beneath her skin, he couldn't discount that possibility.

"There's no need to keep digging at it," he said irritably. "I was convicted for something I didn't do. The Lorr court system is different from Earth's. I had no chance to present a defense. They seem to assume that any evidence given is evidence for conviction."

"So you're not a dangerous man," she said, lowering her eyelids and smiling slightly. "I'm just novaed at that."

"You don't seem mad."

"Let me show you how not-mad I am."

"The ship. Gamma Tertius 4."

"All that will wait. Daddy gave me a ship capable of running without much attention. That's a good thing, because my attention is usually elsewhere."

Lark turned and walked slowly from the cockpit, one hand resting lightly at the neckline of her shimmery, deceptively opaque blouse. Just as she disappeared through the hatchway, the blouse came free and drifted lightly to the control room floor.

Barton Kinsolving bent and picked it up, his

imagination running wild. He had been on the alien prison world for long, dangerous months. And he had been the only human. With the blouse in hand, Kinsolving left the cockpit and followed a trail of discarded clothing to Lark Versalles' sumptuous cabin.

CHAPTER FOURTEEN

"I FIND THIS distasteful in the extreme," Cameron said, nose wrinkling to emphasize his opinion. "Is there no other way to obtain the information?"

"I don't like dealing with Bizzies any more than you do," snapped Kenneth Humbolt, "but this is an extraordinary circumstance."

"Hardly," muttered Cameron. Louder, he said, "Think. These are the creatures who keep humans under their thumb. Such inefficiency they've shown! They cannot keep even a witless wretch like Barton Kinsolving imprisoned."

"Their vaunted prison world seems lacking, doesn't it?" said Humbolt. Only the idea of the aliens' vulnerability sparked a small hint of hope within him. Having to deal once more with Cameron did little to heighten this, though. He did not like the fop, yet the man had his uses.

Humbolt couldn't keep his eyes from darting away from the elegantly dressed Cameron to the small robot hovering at his side. The repulsor field had been turned to low and emitted a barely audible hum, but the deadliness of this machine was apparent in its every line, its every angle. Twin sensors blinked a baleful red like a living predator's eyes. The roving steel wire whips atop its head turned it into a large metallic insect; Humbolt had no idea what those sensors might detect—or if they were sensors.

He shivered slightly at the idea of this robot hunter on his trail. He had seen what it did to the Lorr, but he hadn't witnessed how it had accomplished the dismemberment. Were those antennae heated wires that slashed through flesh? Or had Cameron done something even more diabolical with them? Humbolt's mind ran wild, turning to electric whips and laser cutters and sonic disrupters.

"Discover what the Bizzie knows and I will act upon it," said Cameron. He reached into a brocaded vest pocket and withdrew a small gold box. With one finely manicured thumbnail he flicked open the box. Bending slightly, he put his nose near a tiny tube that had risen from inside. Cameron inhaled sharply and smiled.

"What is that?" Humbolt asked. "I don't want you drugged out of your senses. Kinsolving didn't seem to be the kind to escape from that Bizzie prison, but he obviously did. He might be more dangerous than we think."

"Have no fear, Director Humbolt. This is an innocent enough habit. It contains only pure cerium."

"What?"

Cameron smiled indulgently. "Cerium from your mines on Deepdig."

"You inhale pure rare earths? But those are metals. What—"

"It gives an ineffable response. You really must try it to understand."

"But it's a *metal!*"

"An expensive metal," Cameron pointed out. "Perhaps that is part of its appeal. Not everyone can indulge a gram or two a day. Or perhaps it is the reaction when it reaches the mucous membrane. It dissolves violently in dilute acids."

Humbolt scowled at Cameron, bent over and toggled an intercom switch. "Send the...gentleman in," he ordered.

When the alien walked into the room, Humbolt had to motion Cameron to silence. A second glance at the fop made him power down his robot. The machine had begun a deeper humming and the wire antennae whipped about with the frenzy of a trapped insect.

"Good day. It is kind of you to honor us with your presence, Warden Quonpta." Humbolt almost choked on the alien's name.

"Delete false sentiment," the alien said in a gravelly voice. "I find great trouble in my position. Never before has prisoner escaped. My place at the wardenship is now in question."

"As it should be," muttered Cameron. "You must perform your task well to expect continued tenure."

The alien swung at the waist, his feet remaining firmly fixed on the soft carpet. Twisted at this impossible angle, he said, "You are the hunter?"

"A crude description," said Cameron, smiling. "Think of me as the *man* who will save your reputation."

The emphasis in Cameron's words did not go by the alien unnoticed. He said, "Dealing with space debris such as yourself is similarly ugly to one of my station."

"Gentlemen, please," Humbolt said. "Let's not allow personal differences to cloud the issue. We have mutual interests. Let's explore how to best serve those interests."

"Why do you wish one of your inferior species returned to my planet prison?" Quonpta asked.

"You forget that this 'inferior' species escaped your world," said Cameron with some venom. "No other species has done that, is that not correct?"

"You wish him removed from some larger scheme," the alien went on. "This is the only reason you would consider dealing with me."

"Our reasons," cut in Humbolt, "are our own. If

both your and our reasons are served, where is the controversy?"

"I cannot authorize pursuit," said Quonpta, his gravelly voice turning basso. "We do not have the guards to spare, nor has this matter ever occurred to require such planning."

"I will see to the prisoner's return," said Cameron. "If he tries to find refuge in any human-settled world, I will find him."

"And if he attempts to hide among Biz...among alien populations," said Humbolt, "we require of you a permit for Mr. Cameron to enter those worlds, to pursue and capture."

"Individual worlds relinquish their rights with great difficulty," the alien warden said.

"It won't be easy obtaining the proper documents, you're saying," said Cameron, "but they can be furnished. They *will* be furnished, won't they, Warden?"

Quonpta bobbed his head and flapped long, slender arms as if they were wings. Both men took this to mean agreement.

"Tell us more of the escape," said Humbolt. "We've had only sketchy reports."

"I will not tell you the prison world's location," the alien said.

"We haven't asked. Although we have every hope in the cosmos that no other miscreant of our race is sentenced to this world, we have no desire to meddle in your judicial system, either. If secrecy of the world is part of that system, well..." Cameron spread his hands and smiled wickedly.

"A human starship entered the system, emitting a bogus distress signal."

"What sort of...bogus distress signal?" asked Cameron, his steel-gray eyes now half hooded and his concentration total.

"Engine malfunction. Indications of deliberate

overload were evidenced at many observation spots in the system. The pilot attempted radio communications while in shift space."

"That does seem suspect," said Humbolt. "Everyone knows that isn't possible, that it will cause an infinite drain on engines."

Cameron said nothing.

"The ship vectored directly for planetary landing, using emergency rockets."

"The main stardrive *was* out of commission, then?" asked Humbolt.

"That much is verifiable. Power levels were not at stardrive capability. The ship lands, prisoner Kinsolving enters and our orbiting guard station begins raying."

"Did your laser cannon damage the ship?" asked Humbolt.

"The landing was precise and occurred at the instant when our station could not adequately protect the integrity of our system."

"You're saying, Warden, that the beam dispersion in the atmosphere was so great that the ship escaped damage." Cameron's lips continued to move in silent speech long after he'd made this simple statement.

"That is so. The starship recovered power levels, launched and attained orbit. By the time the guard station had come into position to properly use its weapons, the starship shifted into hyperspace beyond our authority."

"Did you get a launch vector?"

"Inconclusive. There is nothing along that geodesic of hyper-travel. It is our belief that the starship shifted, when only a short distance, recovered orientation in four-space, then shifted toward some other location. The launch from orbit was either done to confuse us or in panic to avoid our laser cannon."

"Either way, they seem to have escaped neatly," said Humbolt. Real admiration rang in his voice. Any triumph over the aliens ranked high in his mind, even if it had been accomplished by one he'd rather see dead.

"Kinsolving's description has been circulated among all races using our prison world. He will find it difficult to escape should he be foolish enough to land on any of them."

"That still leaves human worlds—and those cultures not using your prison world. Which are those?" asked Cameron.

"I am not at liberty to divulge such information. Much of the prison world's efficiency is due to secrecy."

"It won't be secret when Kinsolving sits down and figures out where the world is—but then he already knows, doesn't he? Or someone working closely with him does. It couldn't be an accident that this starship happened by to pick him up."

"That is my thought, Director Humbolt. That is why I come in answer to your summons. If you will seek him, a reward will be offered."

"I ask nothing," said Cameron, "other than the planetary entry permits. Justice will be served."

"Do you hate this Kinsolving so that you send ones like *that* after him?" asked Quonpta of Humbolt.

"Mr. Cameron is a valued employee of Interstellar Materials. He will perform well. Now, Warden, there is one point you have neglected to mention which would be of immense value to us if we are to find Kinsolving."

Human eyes locked with alien. Quonpta finally said, "The recognition signal of the starship was recorded. It is probably false. Why risk such a daring mission and not change your signal?"

"Why have a signal at all?" asked Cameron. His

eyes had closed entirely now. "Why attempt a sneak to a prison world's surface blaring out any recog signal?"

"Here. This means nothing to us. Your registry might aid you."

Quonpta dropped a small metallic disk to Humbolt's desktop. Without another word, the alien warden swung about and left.

Humbolt heaved a deep sigh and settled back in his chair. "Glad he's gone. Those Bizzies give me the creeps."

"Know your enemy," said Cameron. "Consider this. He is panicked enough over Kinsolving's escape to come to Gamma Tertius 4. He came to a human-populated world. I think I can expect my entry permits onto any number of their worlds."

"Only the ones not alerted to Kinsolving's escape," said Humbolt. "Why allow you to duplicate their police forces' efforts?"

"Not so, Director," said Cameron. "The permits will be a mix of worlds. The Bizarres have no desire to make information available to us easily. They might fear we will find out their prison world's true location. Imagine recruiting their criminals for use against them."

"An interesting idea," said Humbolt. "But the danger posed by Kinsolving and the knowledge he carries about the Plan outweighs such speculations."

"What does he know that the Bizzies would believe?"

"Perhaps nothing. We cannot risk *any* leakage to the Bizzies of the Plan. Not at this stage." Humbolt folded his hands across his chest and leaned far back in his chair. "It's a pity we can't recruit Kinsolving."

"Is there any way to burn out his brain and reprogram?" asked Cameron.

"Hardly. The traits in him we'd most like to use would vanish with massive brain-burning. A pity."

"What of the source of his information? What of Ala Markken?"

"It was a lapse on her part," Humbolt said too quickly. "She won't make the same mistake twice."

"She has been rotated back to GT 4, hasn't she? Perhaps attached to your personal staff?" Cameron grinned wickedly.

"That does not concern you. The leak will not recur. Ala is a loyal worker for both IM and the Plan. I suggest that you match her diligence."

"Of course, Director." Cameron picked up the metallic disk left by the alien prison warden. He popped it into a wrist reader. Cameron's eyebrows rose in surprise. "This is an interesting deception on Kinsolving's part," Cameron said. "Such irony I had not expected from him."

"What is it?"

"The registry for the rescuing starship. It's registered to Galaxy Pharmaceuticals and Medical Techtronics."

"Coincidence," snorted Humbolt. "There's no way Interstellar Materials and GPMT could have been tied together in this."

"Unless our Mr. Kinsolving knows more of the Plan than you think."

"Ala doesn't know of GPMT's involvement. Just IM's. This isn't possible."

"Kinsolving appears more dangerous to the Plan than you had thought, Director. Perhaps I should begin my investigation at GPMT." Cameron smiled at the man's obvious discomfort.

"Get Kinsolving. Stop him."

"It would be in our best interests to find out exactly how much he knows of the Plan—and the source of his information. Your, uh, bed companion might know more of the Plan than you do, Director."

"Ala's..." Humbolt cut off his angry retort. Cameron baited him, enjoying the spectacle of a powerful director of Interstellar Materials floundering about.

"I'll start on our valiant, inventive Mr. Kinsolving's trail immediately," said Cameron. "I have a few ideas which might bring him to, uh, *justice*, soon."

Humbolt waved his hand to dismiss Cameron. The man left, the robot tracker following at his heels. Humbolt wished he could activate the robot for just an instant and dispatch Cameron with his own diabolical device.

But he couldn't do that. He needed Cameron. The Plan needed Cameron.

And Kenneth Humbolt needed to have a long talk with Ala. What *had* the woman learned of the Stellar Death Plan—and what had she told Barton Kinsolving?

CHAPTER FIFTEEN

BARTON KINSOLVING found himself talking to an appreciative audience. No matter what he said, even trivial matters dealing with mining, Lark Versalles hung on every word, adoration in her bright blue eyes. And Kinsolving found himself equally fascinated by the lovely woman. As he spoke, her skin tint changed, sometimes dramatically with sharp mood shift, sometimes subtly with highlights of a sparkling dust showing through her translucent skin.

The softer tones that mingled with the more passionate reds and purples he had seen earlier told of her current emotional state—she swung between outright lust for him and a less intense curiosity about his adventures. But both states produced electric, well-defined colors.

"Tell me more," she urged, "about the prison world."

Kinsolving took a deep breath. "The aliens simply drop their convicts on this world. There's not much else to tell."

"To live or die on their own," Lark said breathlessly. She found true fascination in such a sentence. The romance of it—and her part in aiding Kinsolving to escape—flushed her skin with a brighter scarlet and flaring purples that shifted form even as he watched. Kinsolving didn't know if

the woman or her cosmetic dyes intrigued him
more.

"I could never have made it, not even for a week,
without the Sussonssan's help. He kept me alive
long enough to learn how to survive on my own."

"You liked him?"

"I did, in a way. There were others I liked, too, but
I never got to know them as well. It's much like my
professor in graduate school said. The aliens have
different concerns but they are people, too. Learn
what is important to them and they become more
like humans and less...bizarre." This last word almost burnt Kinsolving's tongue. He had heard Cameron use it, and Humbolt, and even Ala Markken.
It had connotations of racial hatred in it that he
couldn't stomach. The short time he'd spent on the
prison world had convinced him that humans and
aliens could live together and even prosper. They
had no designs on humans or human-settled worlds.
They had vast ranges of space for their own, having
been stargoing centuries longer than mankind.

Hadn't he been treated more brutally by his own
kind than by the aliens, especially those like the
toad creature who had unselfishly aided him when
he'd needed it most? It had been Humbolt and Cameron who traded him for the ones responsible for
stealing the ore from Deepdig number two. The
Lorr had only reacted according to their own system
of justice. Even on Earth miscarriages of justice occurred that had nothing to do with racial hatreds.

"Do you know anything about the Plan?" he
asked Lark.

"Plan? Me?" She laughed, the emerald greens in
her cheeks showing sharp spikes as she did so.
"Daddy's always telling me I should plan ahead. I
never do. Maybe I can't. Live for the day. Carpe
diem is the old saying. Why should I bother thinking about the future when the present is so thrill-

ing?" Lark snuggled closer to Kinsolving. "After all, my renegade darling, you've brought more super-charged excitement into my life than anyone in the past six months."

Kinsolving didn't want to ask what Lark had found as exciting as aiding a prison escape. He wasn't sure he could handle it.

"Never mind. I just thought that you might have heard it mentioned. You travel in high circles."

"I *party* in high circles," she corrected. "Business is so boring. Daddy is always telling me I ought to get involved, that he'll start me out in something of my own. Why bother?"

"You can't simply roam the stars forever," Kinsolving pointed out. "You'll need money one day, a job, want to settle down."

"Never!" Lark Versalles denied vigorously. "Daddy'll leave me zillions and zillions, more than I can squander in a dozen lifetimes. Why work when I can do as I please, when I please, no matter where? And 'settling down' sounds more like choosing where I want a grave. There's so much to see and do."

"Parties to attend," Kinsolving said sarcastically.

Lark missed the insult. "Yes! And fun to have." Her cheeks and forehead flushed a light orange that should have been eerie but on Lark wasn't.

He started to protest, but Lark's arms were far stronger than he'd anticipated. She held him down firmly and by the time he wiggled free, he had no real desire to leave her.

"The nav-computer has located four RR Lyrae stars. That's enough to give us a precise fix in space," Kinsolving told Lark.

"We're going to Gamma Tertius 4?"

Kinsolving nodded. That seemed the only route open to him, even though he didn't know exactly what he would do once he arrived at IM's corporate headquarters. From Humbolt he could expect nothing but death. But what of Ala? Would she listen and help him?

"Do you know anyone in the Interstellar Materials hierarchy?" he asked. "Someone who might be able to petition Chairman Fremont for me?"

"I don't know any of the directors," she said almost sadly, "but I know a few of the junior vice presidents." A wicked twinkle came to her eye as she remembered getting to know them. "One of them will do anything I ask. I'm sure of it."

"Who is it?"

"I can't remember his name, but finding him once we get to GT 4 won't be hard. I remember exactly where his office is."

"How did you meet this unknown junior vice president?" Kinsolving asked, even though he didn't want to know the details.

"A corporate party, some sort of celebration about planning for their two hundredth anniversary celebration. Something like that. He struck up a conversation with me and then I—"

Kinsolving yelped as Lark showed him.

"You did that to him in public?"

"No one noticed. We went to his office and continued. He was quite smitten with me. He offered me a job and everything." Lark laughed at the memory. "He didn't know that I could buy and sell him and a million secretaries. I almost offered him a job as *my* assistant, but I thought better of it. No need to rush into anything."

Kinsolving pushed himself free of the woman and her questing hands. The nav-computer had a vector computed for Gamma Tertius 4.

But try as he might, Kinsolving couldn't activate the hyperdrive engines. A single red indicator light flashed whenever he tried. He cursed the "idiot lights" and wished real readouts had been installed to give some clue about the malfunction.

"You told me the lasers hadn't damaged anything seriously," Lark said. "Why aren't we starring off for GT 4? You know how I hate to waste time when there are more fun things happening elsewhere."

"Let me see," Kinsolving said wearily. He toggled the computer and studied the screen as line after line of instruction marched past his eyes. After an hour, he settled back in the chair, eyes strained and his neck muscles bunched. He hadn't even noticed that Lark Versalles had left the cockpit and had now returned.

"Well?" she demanded hotly. "Why isn't this silly ship going anywhere?"

"Safeguards have been built in, Lark," he told her. "We're going to have to make a shift of less than fifty light years to find a space dock that can repair the backup systems. We're limited until we get the emergency rockets refueled and some of those damaged sensors—unimportant though they are—repaired." He tapped out an inquiry and received an instant reply from the nav-computer.

"There's a facility about forty lights away. It's off the geodesic line going to GT 4, which means a longer trip getting there after repairs are finished, but the speedster ought to be up to a hundred and some odd light years."

"I've gone as far as five hundred in one shift," she said proudly. Kinsolving shook his head. Such a distance was reckless. Small errors at launch in the vector turned into monumental errors over five hundred light years. Most travel was accomplished by smaller shifts, often less than twenty light years, with course corrections at every shift back into four-space.

Kinsolving started to give the command to shift to the repair facility, then stopped.

"What's wrong, darling?" Lark asked.

"What am I going to use for money to fix the ship?"

"Oh, silly, don't worry. My credit is good everywhere. What's the world we're shifting to?"

Kinsolving checked. "Upsilon Triangulis 2."

"No need to worry. I know *all* the mechanics there."

Kinsolving didn't doubt her for an instant. He toggled the switch and the speedster surged into hyperspace, following a mathematically precise path through-past-around regular space.

"You *do* know all the workmen," Kinsolving said in amazement. Lark had greeted each one of the men and women by name—and they all seemed to know her, as if she had been gone only a few hours.

"When you travel like I do, it pays to know the people who can put your ship back together. The *Nightingale* doesn't need much work, usually." Lark shrugged. "But sometimes I get impatient and do things like trying to radio from hyperspace. That was dumb. I remember everyone, and I mean *everyone,* telling me I shouldn't do that. But it came out all right." She clung to his arm and rubbed herself against him seductively. "I did meet you, Barton. Anything that lets that happen couldn't be all bad, could it?"

"It might be." Kinsolving stayed in the background, trying not to let the workers see him clearly. He had no idea what hue and cry might go up for him. The aliens had boasted about no one ever escaping from their prison world.

Had anyone made it away and had then been killed? Or was he really the first to ever leave the planet's gravity well alive?

"Sweet ship," one technician said. "Sorry to see Lark abuse her so badly."

"Been rough," Kinsolving said, deciding not replying would attract more attention than speaking.

"Looks as if you've been in a battle. Laser melts on the side. Some of the aluminum exterior has spalled. Sensors overloaded, emergency rocket fuel gone, as if you've been maneuvering heavily." The tech turned and peered hard at Kinsolving. "You're not getting Lark into smuggling, are you?"

The shocked expression on Kinsolving's face made the technician laugh. "That was just a joke. I didn't mean it, though Lark would do anything once just for the experience."

"She's quite a woman," Kinsolving said.

"That she is. But I imagine you've found out in ways I never will." The tech looked around, then dropped into the couch and said in a conspiratorial whisper, "Lark and I did slip off together once. God, what that woman can do with a ten volt battery and some wires! She's a real inspiration to us. Not many ships come into UT 2. Not a one of them has a captain as gorgeous—or willing—as Lark, either."

"I wouldn't think so."

"Where you two headed when you leave?"

Kinsolving held back a sharp retort to tell the man to not ask such personal questions. Instead he said cautiously, "You know Lark. Just launch and wherever the prow points, that's where we go."

"What a life. Envy her. Hell, man, I envy you getting to go along. But you'll burn out. Every man she's ever brought to UT 2 hasn't lasted long. She burns 'em out then finds another. But it's great while it lasts."

Kinsolving nodded and let the technician finish replacing the circuitry under the computer console that had tested bad.

"That's all I can do. If Lark destroys it again, bring it back and let me fix it one more time."

"Can you do the same for me?" Kinsolving asked. The tech laughed and slapped him on the back.

The instant the man left the cockpit, Kinsolving dropped into the couch and began running his own checks on the circuitry. Everything read out perfectly.

"They do such good work, don't they, darling Barton?" asked Lark.

"They do. Let's get going. I don't—" Kinsolving stopped when he saw the burly, armed man with Lark.

"This is Idi. He's station master. He's such a dear. He wanted to check out everything to make sure I'd be all right."

"Your crew did a fine job," Kinsolving said.

"Let me check it out. This is the only way I'll be satisfied." He motioned Kinsolving from the couch. Kinsolving reluctantly vacated so that the huge black man could begin his own examination.

Lark clung to Kinsolving, but the man grew increasingly uneasy. Idi had performed the same circuit check four times; each pass had resulted in a green light indicating nominal performance.

"Why is he stalling?" Kinsolving whispered to Lark.

Her eyebrows shot up and the colors under her skin swirled in crazy eddies. Kinsolving motioned her to silence when Idi's com-link sputtered into life. Kinsolving didn't understand much of what was said, but he caught his name—that was enough to galvanize him into action.

Fists closed and held together, he swung as hard as he could and caught the station master at the base of his massive neck. The jolt rocked Idi forward, but it was Kinsolving's second blow that laid him out on the cockpit deck.

"Why did you do that?" protested Lark. "He's a good friend!"

"I think I broke my hands," moaned Kinsolving. "Help me get him out. Didn't you hear the message that came in over his com-link? He was stalling until he got verification that I was a fugitive."

"Really?" Lark's angry expression faded and sunlight once more shone from her eyes. "How thrilling! We're running from the law! Just like in those old two-dee flickering things that Prinz projects against a wall. They're so silly, but fun!"

Lark helped Kinsolving drag the heavy man to the air lock. On impulse, Kinsolving stripped Idi of the com-link and a small stun tube tucked away inside his shirt so that just the handle had been visible. Then he rolled the man outside and started the lock cycling shut.

"Punch in the coordinates for Gamma Tertius 4," he ordered Lark. "I want an optimum course, minimum time."

"That's the only way I travel." She competently set the controls and let the nav-computer do its job. "This is so photonic!" she enthused. "I'm so happy I met you, Bart darling!"

Kinsolving wasn't convinced that he should allow her to continue with his dangerous mission. Lark had proven useful to this point, but any further might endanger her life. That she reveled in this had nothing to do with it.

But Kinsolving couldn't put her off the *Nightingale*. Not now. Not when the ship's sensors showed building EM fields around the newly repaired hull. The crew at the UT 2 station swung a laser cannon around in an effort to undo all they'd done.

"Hurry," Kinsolving said nervously. "They're getting ready to fire on us. That's their aiming field. That's what is causing the instruments to jump around."

"Don't worry," said Lark. "We'll make it." Her

hand descended to the launch button just as the
starship gave a mighty shudder.

Barton Kinsolving wasn't sure whether they had
shifted into hyperspace or the laser had found its
target.

CHAPTER SIXTEEN

GAMMA TERTIUS 4 throbbed with activity. Even from parking orbit above the desolate world, Barton Kinsolving saw the vitality and energy in the single large city spreading more than ten thousand hectares across the bowl of a gigantic meteor crater. The planet had been airless and worthless to the other starfaring races.

Thaddeus McIntyre had arrived and seen more to the barren rock world than any of the others. His first duty had been to name the tall mountains, one rising at either side of the huge dish-shaped depression in the side of the planet. Mt. Abrupt at the far eastern end was taller than Mt. New Daisy Bates in the west. Then McIntyre set to work with primitive terraforming equipment. Over two hundred years, Interstellar Materials had taken over the work, added sophisticated devices to hold in not only atmosphere but also heat and had transformed the rocky bowl into a miniature paradise.

Kinsolving had been to GT 4 twice. Both times the sight of the green bowl set amid the brown and gray nothingness of the rest of the radiation-wracked world had made him think of Earth and Japanese bonsai trees. A miniature world grew and thrived in the pot of the meteor crater.

"Lovely," he said, not able to take his eyes off the speedster's forward vidscreen.

"Look, Barton darling. There's the corporate

headquarters building. Isn't it cosmic?" Lark fiddled with the vidscreen controls and zoomed in on the two-hundred-story-tall structure of gold and emerald splinters, each segment daring to thrust higher than the last until the upper floors extended beyond the dome of atmosphere and into the vacuum of space. "The entire top floor is executive offices."

Kinsolving tried to imagine the view from there and failed. Situated directly in the center of the huge crater, anyone on that floor had an unsullied view of hundreds of kilometers over the perfectly kept city below.

"That level, level one hundred one, is the party suite. The entire floor!" Lark didn't try to restrain her enthusiasm for once again being at the heart of serious fun.

Kinsolving saw the single flashing light on the control panel. GT Landing Authority needed information before allowing them to leave the *Nightingale*—and Kinsolving couldn't supply it.

He silently indicated that Lark should arrange for transport and care for the speedster while they were below. He swallowed hard and glanced around the small cockpit. He had grown used to the *Nightingale*. Kinsolving smiled ruefully. It hadn't been hard to do, either. Not with every creature comfort imaginable—and not with Lark Versalles aboard.

He knew he might be forfeit if he couldn't contact people willing to plead his case before Chairman Fremont. And even if he succeeded in getting his story to the chairman, that didn't mean Fremont would turn Humbolt and Cameron over to the Lorr for punishment. A director possessed immense power in IM, or any comparably sized off-Earth corporation. Charging Humbolt with the crimes of ore theft and murder and all the rest would cause trouble that might rock Interstellar Materials all the way to the foundations of its immense, beautiful headquarters.

Kinsolving had to rely on Chairman Fremont's integrity to take such risks. He didn't even want to consider the possibility that the rare earths had been stolen on the chairman's orders.

"Hello," Lark called in response to LA's identification request. "Here's the tape on the ship. It has all those silly numbers and things." She played out the registry tape.

"Welcome to Gamma Tertius 4, *Nightingale*," came the immediate response. "How many in your party will be shuttling down to the city?"

"Two," Lark answered without even glancing at Kinsolving. He had wanted her to say only one—he'd risk stowing away to avoid entry procedures. Now his chance for clandestine entry had vanished. "And this time get a *good* pilot. I was here six months ago and the landing was awful. It jarred my teeth it was so rough."

"You must have drawn Bone-breaker Benitez," came the cheerful reply. "We'll see what we can do for you this time. Good, good. How's Chairman Fremont's personal pilot sound? He's landing for the anniversary party, too."

"Oh, photonic! We're in time for it," Lark said. "I don't want to miss a single instant of the parties."

"You're in time, Lark. Treanna's on her way over. You won't have any problems with her landing. Always soft as a lover's touch."

"Thank you, LA." Lark smiled wickedly and toggled the call switch again. "Any chance that you'll be at the party?"

Laughter echoed from the speaker. "Sorry, Lark. No chance. LA's having a party of its own. Nothing as fancy as that on one-oh-one."

"I might come by if the one-oh-one party gets dull."

"Too bad we won't see you," the Landing Authority controller said. "That party'll never get dull. Not if it lasts till the three hundredth anniversary."

To Kinsolving, Lark said, "This is so much fun. I'm glad your orbit crossed mine."

"They'll be looking for me," Kinsolving said, more to himself than to Lark. Then he began to really think. This anniversary party atmosphere might be his saviour, if he proved bold enough to take advantage of it.

"You'll be with me, silly," Lark said, as if this made everything all right. Seeing his expression, she said, "As long as you're with me, who's going to look at you? They'll all be watching *me!*"

Kinsolving had to laugh. "I'm sure they will," he said. "Anyone as lovely as you has to be the center of attention."

"I've got to pack for the party. This Treanna person won't be docking for almost an hour. You keep watch, though, just to be sure. It never pays to keep one of those menials waiting long. I think that's why the landing was so rough last time." With that Lark Versalles vanished, on her way to pack for the anniversary party.

All Kinsolving could do was sit and worry. By the time the shuttle docked and he had helped Lark carry her cosmetics and jewelry cases into the cargo bay, he was keyed up to the point of explosion.

The shuttle down went quickly and smoothly; Kinsolving saw why Fremont had chosen this woman to be his personal pilot. Every move she made at the controls was precise and economical and the landing at the LA field near the edge of the city was over before he noticed they had even begun their final descent.

"All out," Treanna called back. "Don't worry about your cases, Lark. The handlers will take them to your usual suite. We're all glad you could make the party."

Kinsolving shot Lark a startled look. The pilot made it sound as if Lark was more than guest.

"Is your father going to make it?" Treanna asked.

"I don't think so. Daddy is always working so hard. I haven't seen him in over a year now. And he hates to travel."

"We're all happy his daughter doesn't share that trait," Treanna said. "You always brighten any gathering. See you on the way back!"

"Thanks," Lark said, distracted. She drifted from the shuttle, paying no attention to anything going on around her. Kinsolving followed at a discreet three paces, able to see everything and not be intrusive. He tensed as he walked out the passenger tunnel and into the main terminal, expecting armed guards to grab him.

Only the usual bustle of the Landing Authority greeted him. Lark walked through the clearance station without slowing. Kinsolving tried to do the same and was stopped by the clerk.

"Entry visa and travel papers," the clerk demanded. Lark had already vanished, off in search of new thrills, already bored with the bureaucratic demands.

Kinsolving glanced around and decided against using the stun rod he had strapped along his left forearm and hidden by his shirt sleeve. Too many guards prowled the corridors. None had focused on him yet. Any attack on the clerk would draw them like iron filings to a magnet.

"Lost my papers and visa," he said. The clerk's sour expression foretold a long and tedious wait. Kinsolving decided on a bolder approach. He couldn't be in any worse a position for the attempt —and the jumble of data entries might work in his favor. "My name's Barton Kinsolving, supervisor of mines, Deepdig, here as Chairman Fremont's personal guest for the anniversary."

"Supervisor?" the clerk said, one eyebrow rising slightly. "What happened to your papers?"

"That's a long story. I've filed the report with Director Humbolt. Kenneth Humbolt," he said, spelling it for the clerk. "He's my immediate superior." The names Kinsolving tossed around so easily impressed the clerk. Kinsolving thought his heart would explode from the effort of remaining outwardly calm while the clerk entered the data given him.

"Don't have an entry on your visa or travel orders, Supervisor, but the computer is backlogged over a week. The anniversary celebration is bringing in people from Earth and all over."

Kinsolving didn't want to point out that it was longer than this since he'd been convicted by the Lorr. He had taken the chance that Humbolt wouldn't attend to the personnel files himself. If left to any of the subordinates on Deepdig, his records might take months to arrive. Pumping out the mine would require shift-to-shift attention. With the trouble Ala Markken and the others had experienced, he didn't think record updates would rank high on their priorities. And if Ala had been returned to Gamma Tertius 4, that left only decidedly inferior workers in charge.

"Here are duplicates of your identicard and papers, Supervisor. You'll have to verify first. Press your hands here. Good. And for the dupes I need your retinal pattern, too."

Kinsolving lowered his face to the soft-covered ocular and blinked as the laser scanned his left eye and matched it with records hidden deep in the corporate computer. He heaved a sight of relief when no bells went off, when no guards came running after him.

"Have a great time, Supervisor."

"Thanks." Kinsolving turned to follow the course Lark had taken.

"Supervisor!" Kinsolving froze in his tracks. He slowly turned to face the clerk. "The blond woman that went through with Absolute Clearance. Was she with you?"

"Yes," Kinsolving said cautiously.

"Nothing," the clerk said. The expression of lust and envy on his face told the story. Kinsolving didn't have to be a telepath to know what the clerk's thoughts were, either. *Lucky bastard*, had to run through his mind.

Barton Kinsolving had acted with boldness and won. The company computer hadn't yet been flagged to record any use of his name or identicard. Until such time, he could live well and devote his full attention to reaching Chairman Fremont.

Kinsolving felt a cold wind across his spine as the thought came to him that the computer might be updated at any time. When it was, any use of his identicard would bring down company guards in droves.

He pushed the worry aside. If he dwelled on it, he might accomplish nothing. Courage had carried him this far. Courage would get him to Fremont and total absolution.

Outside the LA terminal, Kinsolving simply stood and breathed the fine, pure, cool air. A gentle wind blew from the north. That meant it was late afternoon. Every five hours, the direction of the wind changed by ninety degrees in a clockwise pattern, returning to any given direction exactly one GT day later. Kinsolving walked a few paces and turned. At his back rose Mt. Abrupt. In the far distance, hidden by the gleaming shaft of the headquarters building would be Mt. New Daisy Bates. Having his bearings, Kinsolving hailed a passing car, used his identicard and told the robot, "Supply."

He settled back as the quick spurt of acceleration thrust the car through traffic and toward the company warehouse. He needed more than a single change of clothing if he wanted to present a good appearance at Interstellar Materials' anniversary party.

Completely outfitted, he charged the bill against his accrued salary. Every use of his identicard caused Kinsolving to tense but the use was always authorized.

He knew it couldn't continue much longer. He had to reach Fremont—soon.

Going directly to the headquarters building with his newly packed cases, he entered the main lobby and looked around. Only once before had he been here. Then he'd had a guide to usher him up to the appropriate corporate office. Without such a guide, he didn't have any idea how to proceed.

He went to an information counter and toggled the Attention switch.

"How may IM be of service?" came the computer-generated voice. He had asked in one of his college courses why the information 'bots were never equipped with truly human-sounding voices. The professor had chuckled at the notion.

"Humans love being served," had been the answer. "You can dominate a robot, abuse it, insult it, walk away and feel better. A human treated similarly will make certain your request is never granted—or will be granted in the longest possible time."

"Efficiency," Kinsolving muttered.

"All IM employees strive for efficiency," came the robotic voice.

"I'm looking for Lark Versalles. She has a suite."

"That information is secured."

"I have some of her cases. Not all were delivered," Kinsolving said, changing his tack. The computer didn't care; a human would. Another count for machine over man when trying to dodge the system's rules.

"Leave them at the service entrance, northwest side, entry port five."

"They must be carried by hand. I will do it."

Kinsolving waited for the computer to make the proper decision. "One moment, please, while I contact the suite."

"Barton?" came Lark's immediate cry from the speaker. "Is that you? Where did you go?"

"Give me the entry code. I'm in the main lobby." Kinsolving looked around, certain that he would be detected at any instant. The feeling of paranoia grew inside until he wanted to scream. He felt exposed and was sure that every passing person would turn and point at him and begin to yell for guards.

"I'm on level forty-seven. Go to the lift shafts at the far side of the lobby and just give my name."

"You used your name as entry code?"

"Oh, don't be like that, darling. Daddy always chides me about such things. I know better, but it's so hard remembering silly codes and all that. This way I never forget and lock myself out and get embarrassed. Do hurry. It's so . . . lonesome in this big suite."

"Be right up," he assured her. Before he left the service robot, he said, "Send my cases to suite code Lark Versalles."

"Right away, sir." The tiny pop indicated that the order had been transmitted even as he gave it.

Kinsolving heaved a sigh of relief as he hurried across the wide marble-floored lobby. His fears had turned out to be irrational. So far everything had gone well.

He reached the elevators and pressed the summons button, stood back and waited.

The door opened—and out strode Cameron, a robot hunter-killer humming along on its repulsor field at his side.

CHAPTER SEVENTEEN

BARTON KINSOLVING felt the blood rush from his head. The dizziness assailing him turned into advantage. He turned to one side, hand hiding his face. Kinsolving bent over and went to one knee, facing away from Cameron. The man stopped; Kinsolving waited for the hand on his shoulder, the nerve-jangling impact of a stun rod, the shouted cry for guards, the robot to attack.

It did not come.

"Are you well?" Cameron asked.

"Too much t'drink," Kinsolving said, slurring. "Wunnderful party."

Cameron sniffed. "I dare say you've outlived your invitation at any party I wish to attend." The overdressed man snapped his fingers and the hunter robot attentively followed.

Kinsolving chanced a look up to see the brightly dressed Cameron vanish in the crowded lobby. For long seconds, Kinsolving couldn't stand. His legs were too weak and shaky. He finally took a deep breath and forced calm on himself. He had almost come face-to-face with the man responsible for his woes. That he still lived spoke as much of pure luck as it did skill.

Kinsolving didn't lie to himself about escaping Cameron. Surprise had to be a major element. No one would expect a fugitive to return to the source of corporate power. And Kinsolving had to admit that Cameron and Humbolt might not even know he'd escaped from the prison world. Would the aliens sound an alarm and warn the human worlds —especially Gamma Tertius 4—of his singular escape?

He took a quick glance into the elevator cage and saw that it was empty. Only then did he enter and touch the code switch and say, "Lark Versalles."

The sudden rise of the cage drove him to his knees. Clumsily standing, Kinsolving was glad that he was alone. Explaining such behavior would be difficult—and it would make him memorable. The last thing he wanted now was to be memorable.

"Think small, think insignificant," he told himself.

The doors opened and all attempts to be insignificant vanished. A robutler hovered near the opened elevator door and said, "Welcome Master Barton. Lady Lark awaits you in her suite."

In addition to the robot, several human servants stood impassively along the walls, waiting for the slightest hint of need. Kinsolving tried not to gawk as he trailed behind the robutler. The carpets had to be Persian. No other design and texture felt this way beneath his feet. Paintings from renowned artists decorated the walls, with tasteful statuary placed so that the lines broke in unexpected spots. Most of all, the area was dominated by the panoramic view from the diamond-clear windows over the city, dots and squares of green betraying parks and browns and grays showing buildings.

Kinsolving walked along in a daze of wonder at such wealth. His prior visit to GT 4 hadn't revealed this aspect of Interstellar Materials' operations. He knew that he had blundered into a world reserved for only a select few.

A select few like Lark Versalles.

"Darling!" the woman greeted him. She threw her arms around his neck and swung him about as he walked into a room even more expensively decorated than the area outside. He hardly noticed the room's furnishings. Lark was gorgeously nude and outshone even the most cleverly contrived artwork.

"Do you like it?" she asked, bouncing away from him to display the canvas of her bare skin. "I had some of the dyes redone and intensified the colors in others." Nipples gleamed a bright blue, then faded to gray-blue, only to change into hues Kinsolving couldn't put a name to. Her breasts changed shades to stay complementary to her nipples, and the rest of her body coloring writhed with a pseudolife that took away his breath.

"Fantastic," he murmured.

"I knew you'd like it. But do hurry. We've got a reception to attend. Not a big one, just a few hundred of the *top* IM execs."

"Lark, wait," he began.

"You're not going to vanish on me again, are you? That was rude, disappearing like you did at the LA." She stamped her foot in mock anger. The action of foot against carpet caused jagged edges of coloration to rise in her left calf.

"I had to get some papers," he said. "My identi-card." He swallowed and tried to look her squarely in the eye. The effort proved almost more than Kinsolving could achieve. The spectacle of her body drew him powerfully, as it was designed to.

"But now that you've got all that you want," Lark started.

"The party," he said. "Who is going to be there? I've got to make contact quickly. If I don't..." Kinsolving let the words trail off as he remembered the chance encounter with Cameron in the lobby. The man might have been dressed like some courtier from eighteenth century France, but Kinsolving remembered the look on his face when he killed the Lorr agent-captain. Cameron had enjoyed it, truly *enjoyed* the murder. Behind that fancy exterior lay a cold and cunning mind.

"Oh, you can be such a bother," Lark said in exasperation. "Just about everyone will be there. Don't worry, my darling. I'll introduce you to someone who can help. I promise." With that, she spun, lifted elegantly on one toe to accentuate the muscles in her legs and send new patterns arrowing up along those slender calves, then dashed off to dress.

Kinsolving collapsed into a chair and simply stared out across the city. He ought to be enjoying the promise of Interstellar Materials' two hundredth anniversary. For the past hundred years the company had been on GT 4 making this small segment of the world into paradise.

Kinsolving looked at the city and saw only bleakness. His life lay shattered and the only hope of piecing it together again was dressing in the next room, more intent on choosing the right gown than helping him. Kinsolving shook his head. He shouldn't complain. If it hadn't been for the chance landing of the *Nightingale* he would never have escaped the alien prison.

Coldness clamped his heart. Had Lark's arrival been pure chance? Did Humbolt plan something more for him, something even more diabolical than incriminating him in murder and theft?

Kinsolving couldn't figure out what that might be. But one question that he'd never had a chance to ask did come to mind. He called out, "Lark, will you answer a question?"

"Certainly, darling, if you'll tell me which you prefer. This one or this awful blue monstrosity."

Kinsolving spun in the chair. Lark had turned on the glamour mirror and stood before it naked. Reflected was her face and lush body clothed in a scintillating rainbow of electricity. The fabric seemed to be more plasma than solid, shifting and shining, glowing and hiding.

"This? Or this?" She touched the frame of the glamour mirror and the rainbow vanished, replaced by a blue gown that seemed plain in comparison.

"The blue," he said without hesitation.

"But it doesn't *do* anything," Lark protested.

"What will the other women be wearing?"

The blonde smiled slowly as she understood. "Oh, yes, I knew there was a reason I brought you along." She danced over to him, bent and kissed him lightly on the lips.

"Lark, the question, Who is your father? Why does IM give you such a lavish welcome?"

"Daddy's so rich, he could buy and sell Interstellar Materials a dozen times over. That's why they fawn all over me. They're afraid I might say something nasty and then he'll actually buy them out."

"He's a stockholder?"

"Hardly. Don't repeat this, but Daddy would never have anything to do with a company whose revenue came from grubbing in the dirt. Nothing against you, darling Barton, but you must admit that it *is* rather primitive."

"But—" The door chimes interrupted Kinsolving. He sank down in the chair, letting the back hide him as the robutler glided over to answer.

"Lady Lark," the machine said, "the summons for the party has come. The opening presentations will be made in exactly five minutes."

"Oh, and I don't have anything to wear."

"The blue dress," Kinsolving said.

Lark touched the frame twice, then tugged at the glamour mirror's edge to reveal a cabinet. Inside hung the blue dress, specifically tailored to the measurements recorded in the mirror. Lark hurriedly dressed. Kinsolving hadn't thought the woman capable of such speed. She took his arm and almost dragged him from the room.

"We've got to be on time for the opening. That's when I'll be able to see who I can contact in your behalf." She squeezed tightly on his arm and guided him toward the elevator. The robutler obediently held the ornately wrought doors open. Again the sudden acceleration almost drove Kinsolving to his knees.

Before he could speak, the doors slipped away to show level one-oh-one and the party goers already filling the immense room.

"Time to go to work," Lark said, laughing. She pulled him forward and immediately began greeting elegantly dressed men and women in dresses so dazzling Kinsolving worried that he might need polarized goggles to keep from squinting. A few he recognized as junior executives at IM—he prayed that they didn't recognize him.

But Kinsolving need not have worried. If he stayed with Lark Versalles, he would never be the center of attention.

He quickly found, though, that he couldn't stay beside her. Not when the men clustered around her forced him away. He silently drifted to one wall and clung there, eyes scanning the party for anyone he might approach. A few junior vice presidents were in attendance but he didn't see Humbolt—or Cameron. He had hoped to find Chairman Fremont, but the frail man was nowhere to be seen.

Kinsolving hung back during the opening ceremonies. This was the first party of a month-long celebration IM planned to celebrate two hundred years of business off Earth.

"Friends of Interstellar Materials," a dark, pretty woman said from a small stage in the center of the room. "Welcome. Chairman Fremont regrets that health has prevented him from attending today, but he has entrusted me with the joyous duty of dedicating this status of Thaddeus McIntyre, the illustrious architect and builder of our headquarters, the man whose vision and foresight took us away from the planet of our origins and carved out a niche on Gamma Tertius 4."

The woman spoke of happiness and light, but a coldness about her made Kinsolving think of icebergs and the hard vacuum of deep space.

"Who is she?" he asked a woman standing by him.

"That's Director Villalobos."

Kinsolving said nothing more. Maria Villalobos was often mentioned as Fremont's successor. He had never seen her before, much less met her—but her presence convinced him that she was not the proper one to plead his case. The cold light from her eyes made it obvious that Cameron wasn't the only person at IM without scruples.

He might be doing Villalobos a disservice, but he didn't think so. Kinsolving looked around in time to see Lark leaving, arms linked with a young man dressed in an old-style tuxedo. Kinsolving started after them, then stopped. He didn't know what he would be interrupting—but he could guess.

Trying not to look too uncomfortable, Kinsolving floated around the periphery of the crowd. He felt a sense of forced merriment about them. These young IM executives were here for business, not pleasure. They worked one another, jockeying for power and influence, seeking information to use for profit and blackmail. Kinsolving watched in a mood approaching awe, remembering similar parties he had attended. His own actions hadn't been much different. Although he was a damned good engineer, he wasn't expert enough to be made supervisor at his age without also being good at trading information and influence.

He marvelled that he had once played this game. Kinsolving was now an outside observer; all was apparent to him. If only he didn't have to find someone to clear him, he might have enjoyed this revelation.

Some social sense caused him to jerk about in time to see Lark returning with the man. They parted and she quickly went to the side of another, older man. Kinsolving knew that Lark enjoyed this party, as much for the sexual opportunities it afforded as for the contact with wealth and power.

He moved quickly to within a few paces. The man she spoke to seemed familiar. When Kinsolving heard the blonde's words, he recognized his chance.

"Oh, Director Liu, this is such a *fine* party. You planned it, didn't you?"

The director of IM's financial division basked in Lark's praises. Within ten minutes, they left, Lark's fingers toying with the fastrip at the front of Liu's pants. The director playfully batted her hand away, but not too hard, not enough to discourage her.

Kinsolving followed at a discreet distance.

"Director, can we go to your office? I would ever so like to see it."

"No, Lark, not there. It's at the top of the building. Even with my private elevator, it would take too long to get there. I want you, my lovely. Now!"

Lark squealed in joy as Liu pushed her into a

small, intimately lit room. Kinsolving moved quickly, fingers curled around the edge of the door to keep it from closing and locking. He didn't have to worry about Liu or Lark seeing him. They were intent only on each other.

Kinsolving's uneasiness at watching vanished when he saw Lark toss the director's jacket across the room. It hit the floor with a dull thud that told Kinsolving something bulky was hidden away in a pocket. When the pair fell to the immense bed and began serious lovemaking, Kinsolving crept along the wall to where the jacket lay. He fumbled in the pocket and found a secure-case holding the director's identicard and at least a dozen other entry cards.

Kinsolving took the secure-case and left the room. It would be at least a half hour before Liu noticed the theft. If the man's power appealed enough to Lark, it might be longer than that. Kinsolving found another small room and went inside. It took him almost fifteen minutes to break open the secure-case and pull out the identicard. He pocketed it. The other cards were clearly marked for the security areas they granted access to.

All except one blank card. At first Kinsolving thought it was a spare Liu carried, one to be electronically imprinted. But his fingers ran along the edge and felt the dull nicks in the plastic. The card had been used often.

Kinsolving didn't worry about it. He sat down on the edge of a chair and thought about his windfall in obtaining these entry card keys. Somewhere within the IM computer must lie evidence that could clear him. Ala Markken had claimed that her thefts of the rare earth oxides had been condoned by someone higher up. He had assumed that she meant Kenneth Humbolt.

With Director Liu's identicard and access card

keys, Kinsolving hoped to be able to prove that. With evidence against Humbolt, he might be able to clear himself of the murder charges, also.

If nothing else, he could prove to Chairman Fremont that he had nothing to do with stealing from the company—and that the true culprit was still seated on the board of directors.

Barton Kinsolving left the room, seeking the executive elevators that would take him to Director Liu's office and the computer access available there.

CHAPTER EIGHTEEN

BARTON KINSOLVING thrust the stolen identi-card into the receptor slot near the elevator. For a moment, he imagined alarms sounding in the heart of the headquarters building, armed guards rushing out to capture him, a million overlooked details tripping him up.

The doors silently slid open to reveal a spacious room; Kinsolving hesitantly advanced. The doors slid shut behind him. Only then did he realize this *was* an elevator.

"Floor?" came a soft voice. Kinsolving spun around, seeking the source of the sound.

He laughed ruefully. He had always wanted robot voices to sound human; he had railed about the information center in the lobby sounding so mechanical. The directors of Interstellar Materials shared his distaste and for their private use had programmed the computer properly.

"Director Liu's office," he said.

"May I check the authorization pass?" the computer asked. A single wall panel glowed a dull, cool blue in anticipation of reading the pass.

"This is a direct order. Take me to the director's office."

"Please, sir. I have been ordered to inquire of any unescorted passengers using this elevator."

Kinsolving glanced at the closed door and knew that he would be trapped if he couldn't produce the proper card key. He pulled out the stack of cards stolen from Liu and flipped through them, wondering which, if any, would be an appropriate pass.

A light blue card matching the panel seemed a good choice. He touched it to the panel and the light immediately vanished. The computer said, "Thank you, sir. Sorry for the inconvenience."

"Security is important," he said, wiping sweat from his forehead.

"I am happy you understand, sir."

Even before the computer had finished the apology, the doors slid open to show the directors' suites. Kinsolving left the elevator, cautiously checking every cross corridor. The anniversary celebrations had taken the staff from their usual posts. For that, Kinsolving heaved a deep sigh of relief. A stolen key card might get him past an elevator computer but it wouldn't work with a human guard or curious staff member.

Kinsolving wandered the lavishly decorated halls until he came to a door with Liu's name inlaid in gold and rubies. Using the identicard gained him entry.

He sat down in the chair behind the broad desk and shook. He wasn't used to breaking and entering. The strain of being keyed and ready for flight at the slightest noise had worked a toll on him both physically and emotionally.

Kinsolving settled his nerves and swung about in the plush chair and stared out over the city. This level of the gold and emerald building rose above the dome of atmosphere contained in the bowl of the crater. The ebon starkness of space allowed the stars to shine, even in midday, with diamond hardness.

"To work here," he muttered.

"May I be of service?" came the immediate response from a hidden computer.

"Yes. I need to view company files."

Kinsolving sat back when a computer console rose from the bare desktop. He moved the chair closer and hesitantly tapped at the keys. Surprise blossomed when he found that he didn't have to enter an access code. Liu was Comptroller of Interstellar Materials and had all financial records at his fingertips. Kinsolving realized again how lucky he had been to get into this office. The computer hadn't required passwords because of the impossibility of anyone reaching this point without being detected and stopped.

He jumped at every slight noise made in the outer offices. Kinsolving worked quickly, not sure what he wanted. From time to time he took notes on all that he found in the records of liftings from Deepdig. Other inquiries showed that the Deepdig shipping records had been altered to reflect not what had been lifted but what remained after a considerable portion had been stolen.

He found no evidence to show that Humbolt had been responsible. From the records available to Liu, he couldn't even show theft had occurred.

"If nothing is obvious, then they can't come back and say I was responsible. Whoever has stolen the ore has done a great job of covering up."

"Theft, sir?" came the attentive computer voice.

"Cancel," he said quickly.

Only the Lorr charge of murder appeared to be of any significance. That Kinsolving considered a mixed blessing. He had only this charge to disprove to clear his name. But proving his innocence would be difficult—more so if he couldn't show why Humbolt or Cameron would want to make it look as if he had committed the crime.

No theft, no motive to frame him.

He finished his probing with a complete listing of

destinations for the refined rare earths. He cursed
under his breath as he handwrote all he saw on the
console screen. Daring to ask for a hard copy might
be his undoing if a notation were made internally.
He doubted screen access would trigger such a
counter.

He hoped that it wouldn't.

"Finished," he said, standing. He had been here
too long and had gained little for his effort. Kinsolving went back to the elevator, lost in thought.
He entered the spacious room, then looked up when
the computer again asked for access card.

Once more the panel glowed a light blue, but this
time Kinsolving accidentally pressed the unmarked
card against it.

The elevator dropped precipitously, then came to
a halt amid a mechanical grinding that made him
worry about the machinery's safety.

"Is anything wrong?" he asked.

"Secured entry permitted," the computer said.
Kinsolving stiffened when the computer added, "All
success to the Plan!"

The doors opened. Kinsolving looked at the panel
indicator inside the elevator but nothing showed.
He poked his head out and looked around. The directors' offices had been luxurious beyond even a sy-
barite's dream. This floor proved as plain as an
Earth office. Kinsolving slipped from the elevator
and looked around.

No secretaries' desks lined these halls. No indication of any staff hinted at the importance of the few
offices he found. Kinsolving looked into one office. It
was almost empty. The next he found in similar
condition. The last five had desks and computer
consoles, but nothing as elaborate as that in Director Liu's office.

If the computer voice hadn't mentioned this mysterious "Plan" Kinsolving would have believed that

a malfunction had dropped him onto a floor populated by minor, insignificant functionaries.

The office appearing to be used most drew him. He sat in the chair and tentatively touched the keys on the computer console. The screen glowed phosphorescently.

"What is the access code? Or is there one?" he asked, then clamped his mouth shut, waiting for the answering office robot. No robot. No sounds except for the distant creaks of the building heating and cooling. Kinsolving glanced out the window and saw that the view from the crystal windows was obscured by turbulence. This strange grouping of offices was positioned at the boundary layer between the dome of atmosphere sheltering the city and the harshness of space, almost as if by plan.

Plan. The Plan. *The* Plan.

Kinsolving worked at the console. His first attempts produced only restricted notations. Some codes were required, but general access had to gain him more information than he now had.

Under his breath, he mumbled as he worked. "What *is* the Plan?" he asked, putting this question to the computer, not expecting a response—and astounded when it began rolling across the screen.

Kinsolving sat back and read as fast as he could. The words reeled by with the precision of marching soldiers and he missed much, but he got more than he'd hoped.

Frantically, he scribbled notes on a scrap of paper. Again he wished he could send his captured output to hard copy, but that was out of the question. Kinsolving wondered that he hadn't set off alarms all over the building. Then he smiled wanly. The people responsible for the Stellar Death Plan wouldn't want to alert anyone else to their subversion, to their misuse of IM property.

He settled back and held his head between shaking hands when the scrolling had stopped. He knew where the stolen rare earth oxides had been shipped, how they had been stolen—and their purpose. He shivered all over at the magnitude of the Plan.

"Who's responsible?" he wondered aloud. "Who?" Nowhere in his search did he discover a listing of those at Interstellar Materials instituting such a diabolic plan for mass alien destruction.

A slight sound from the corridor alerted Kinsolving. He leaped from the chair and raced to the door. He pressed his ear against the panel but heard nothing. Kinsolving pulled the door open slowly against its mechanism until a slit allowed him a view of the hallway.

His heart almost stopped at the sight. Cameron patrolled the hall, his robot hunter hovering at his knee. As Kinsolving watched, the gaudily dressed man paused, head tipped to one side as if listening. Cameron turned ninety degrees, reached out and opened an office door.

"Go!" the man cried. The robot hunter dazzled Kinsolving with the speed of its departure. One instant it hung at Cameron's side, the next it simply vanished. He had no desire to find out its other capabilities.

He evaluated his chances. If he stayed, Cameron would find him. The tracking senses of the robot must be acute—why it hadn't already found him hardly mattered. It would. Soon.

Kinsolving acted before he thought through the consequences. He left the relative safety of the office and dashed into the hall. Cameron heard and spun to his right. Kinsolving's fist found the fop's nose. Kinsolving felt cartilage crushing and warm blood spurting. Cameron strangely did not emit any sound. He shifted weight and tried to counter, but Kinsolving still had the advantage. Instinctively, he used it. A hard shoulder caught Cameron high on the chest and sent the man reeling back into the office being investigated by his robot hunter.

Cameron crashed to the floor, momentarily shaken. Kinsolving slammed the office door and fumbled, finding his blank card. He pressed it into the key slot. A soft "snick" signaled the door locking.

Heart racing and breath coming in ragged gasps, Kinsolving stumbled back and dived into the waiting elevator.

"Your identicard is required, sir," came the soft, polite, human-sounding voice.

"Main lobby," he said, presenting Liu's blank card—the card that had unlocked the Stellar Death Plan for him.

"Thank you, sir." Kinsolving gasped at the speed of descent. He tumbled into the lobby, but no one noticed. They were too intent on their holiday, their own celebration of Interstellar Materials' two hundredth anniversary.

Barton Kinsolving had no idea where he ran, but he knew he had to get away from the headquarters, from Cameron, from the robot that would soon be sent after him.

CHAPTER NINETEEN

BARTON KINSOLVING tried to control his burgeoning fear. The thought of Cameron's deadly robot hunter coming after him made him want to run and run and run. To do so would attract unwanted attention. At points around the huge lobby stood corporate security guards. Their function was more ceremonial than enforcement, but Kinsolving didn't doubt that they would spring into action if Cameron—or any IM director—ordered them after a fugitive.

He was the fugitive. And he felt the pressure of time. He had rifled the files of Interstellar Materials and stolen a director's entry card keys. Those two crimes would send him to prison on Gamma Tertius 4, but Kinsolving knew that would be preferable to spending the rest of his life on the alien prison world.

But prison wasn't where he would end up if Cameron caught him. After reading the brief summary of their Stellar Death Plan in the tiny offices sandwiched between corporate floors, he posed more danger to them alive than he did dead.

"Who are they?" he muttered.

"Sir?" asked a guard. "Did you say something?"

"Nothing. Just talking to myself."

The guard eyed him curiously. Kinsolving swore under his breath. He hadn't wanted to attract attention. Now this guard would remember him when questioned. Kinsolving hurried from the lobby and stood looking directly west at the craggy spire of Mt. New Daisy Bates turning ochre in the rays of the too-distant setting sun. Did the rim wall around the city hold sanctuary for him?

Kinsolving didn't think so. The area encompassed by this artificial city had seemed immense when he had landed. Now it constricted, squeezed in on him, made him feel that there wasn't any room to run. With IM owning everything in the city—and on Gamma Tertius 4—he had no one to turn to. Everyone worked for the company in some capacity, even the smallest shop owner in the commercial section.

Most owed considerable devotion to Interstellar Materials, too, for getting them off overcrowded Earth, away from the pollution and ruin, and for giving them jobs.

Kinsolving held his head, feeling as if it would explode. His temples pounded like an ocean surf and the arteries in his throat throbbed and cut off his wind. He had to escape, he had to hide, he had to think.

Walking aimlessly would only work against him. Kinsolving took a few seconds and decided that a park provided the best chance for concealment. Anywhere that he might stay away from prying eyes gave Kinsolving that much more hope.

The park system of GT 4 had been designed by experts to give the maximum amount of privacy in the smallest possible space. The greenery helped the city air supply to a small degree, but oxygen and other gases for the atmosphere were artificially generated.

Kinsolving walked slowly along a path, then left it, going across a grassy sward to a rocky alcove with a scenic view of a tiny waterfall and stream meandering through the park. From this vantage he could see most approaches without being obvious. He settled down and tried to work out a real escape.

Leaving Gamma Tertius 4 would be dangerous. Cameron would immediately close off the Landing Authority. He probably knew who he hunted—Kinsolving now believed that the aliens would have alerted IM about the escape from the prison planet. Even if Cameron had no idea who had broken into the Plan offices and struck him, the LA would be closed down tight. That might prove a problem for IM in a few days when many of the guests started to leave the parties to return to their duty stations out-space. Until then, the LA could admit anyone coming in from off-planet and not seem restrictive.

Or did anyone on GT 4 care about such things? The company ruled the planet. Would they meekly abide by any corporate decision, no matter how oppressive or in violation of Earth law?

Such as destroying entire planets and their alien populations? Kinsolving shuddered at what he had found in the computer files. The Stellar Death Plan was nothing less than a blueprint for genocide on a scale undreamed of before. A few million had died at the hands of Earthly dictators.

Those fostering the Stellar Death Plan had grander and bloodier dreams.

They would slaughter alien races down to the last individual. And, from what Kinsolving guessed, they wouldn't stop with just one. They wanted *all* aliens dead. The paranoia about other species he had heard in Kenneth Humbolt's words had been translated into action on a scale so vast Kinsolving wanted to think it was all a gigantic prank being played on him.

He knew it wasn't. The look on Cameron's face when he murdered the Lorr agent-captain proved graphically that this was no joke. Cameron had wanted to kill the alien, had *enjoyed* it.

Kinsolving's mind rolled and turned and spun and came up with no idea what he should do. Even escaping GT 4 would prove difficult. If he didn't, the best he might hope for would be death. The worst? Return to the alien prison world. Kinsolving had to chuckle at that thought, though. Cameron and Humbolt would be certain that he never left Gamma Tertius 4 alive.

Not after he had seen the broad outline of their vicious, racist Plan.

"What alien would believe me if I told them?" Kinsolving said aloud. The answer had to be simple: none. He had been convicted of killing a Lorr, a crime viewed as extreme by the aliens. They would assume he concocted details of the Plan to escape punishment.

Kinsolving stood and paced around the small rock enclosure, trying to find a way out, a way to alert the aliens to their danger without bringing horrendous retribution down on Earth and all humans, a way of stopping Humbolt before he carried out his savage scheme.

An electric tension in the air caused Kinsolving to stop his nervous movements and peer hard toward the entrance to the park. He saw only a few pedestrians walking slowly, some hand in hand. This was all he saw, but the man *felt* far more.

He knew in that instant how prey felt when sighted by a hungry predator.

Kinsolving held down the impulse to bolt and run for his life. Common sense prevailed. If he did, whoever sought him would be able to pinpoint him instantly. Who else in the park ran? Who else would emit the sweat of fear and the stench of panic?

He climbed to the top of the rocky cul-de-sac and got a better view of the trails leading to his high point. Kinsolving went into shock when he saw Cameron and his robot hunter slowly following his path up the hill. The robot swayed to and fro, as if swinging on a spring. The far end of each deviation from the path caused it to bob and bounce, then it returned, to repeat the procedure on the far side. It checked for spoor, both visual and odorous.

Did it also have sound and motion detectors? Could it hear the frenzied beating of his heart? See the way his chest throbbed under his shirt?

Kinsolving calmed. It was a machine and nothing more. Its senses might be enhanced, more acute than any human's, but it required constant programming. Without Cameron tending it, the robot hunter was nothing. Nothing but a dumb machine.

The fear remained but it no longer paralyzed him. Kinsolving started to plot how best to eliminate Cameron. The flashes off his bright clothing from the rays of the setting sun turned to blood before they reached Kinsolving. The man vowed that it would be Cameron's blood, not his own, spilled this day. Hadn't he already broken the man's nose?

That might anger Cameron, cause him to make mistakes he wouldn't normally. Kinsolving could only hope.

Seeing the way Cameron advanced, however, dashed any hope of the predator becoming careless because of rage. Cameron walked slowly along the path paying no attention to his robot hunter. His eyes scaled the heights for any trace of his prey. Once Kinsolving saw the man stop and cock his head, listening hard.

Cameron put his hands on his hips and rocked back, yelling, "There is no need to be tedious about this, Supervisor Kinsolving. Please come out. I bear you no malice for damaging my nose." Cameron reached up and ran his finger along its straight, hawkish length. "I've already gotten it tended to. Come down and let's talk."

He appeared foppish, but Kinsolving had seen

him kill without remorse. What weapons did Cameron have hidden? Kinsolving almost laughed aloud at his own stupidity. What weapon did Cameron need when he had that robot hunter coursing back and forth?

"Weapon!" Kinsolving exclaimed. He had forgotten the stun rod he'd stolen so long ago. He fumbled about inside his shirt and found the slender rod. Pulling it out and holding it gave him a small thrill of advantage. But he knew next to nothing about such things. What was its range? Glancing down at Cameron, he estimated the distance to be greater than a hundred meters. Kinsolving didn't want to test the weapon in this fashion.

"Supervisor?" came Cameron's call. "My robotic friend has your track now. It would have worked quicker except that it had no scent to compare with the trail. Now that it does, it will be able to follow you through even the densest population. Crowds will not shelter you or confuse my robotic friend, Mr. Kinsolving. Make it easy on yourself. Come down and let's talk."

From robot hunter's homing motions, Kinsolving knew that Cameron wasn't lying. The machine had found his scent and now worked quickly to close distance. Kinsolving scrambled down the far side of the hill, out of breath by the time he reached the bottom. Only open grassy meadows stretched in front. The curvature of the hill on either side offered scant protection.

Or did it? The robot would not attempt to outguess him. It would follow his track exactly, no matter how he dodged. In that might be his salvation.

Taking the rockier side, Kinsolving began working his way around the hill, slowing when he came to the side where Cameron had stood. The man had advanced in the wake of his robot hunter. Something warned Cameron. He pulled out a heavy rod—a weapon Kinsolving didn't recognize. Cameron started to circle the hill, as if he had some hint of what Kinsolving had done.

Kinsolving could run. Both robot and master would take long minutes to find what he had done. But that gained Kinsolving nothing. Flight only prolonged the inevitable.

He attacked.

Stun rod in hand, he started directly up the slope after the robot hunter. He hoped that Cameron had ranged far enough not to hear his somewhat clumsy assault.

Cameron didn't; the robot did. The metallic insect swung about its axis, repulsor field whining slightly with the exertion. Thin whips lashed back and forth like obscene antennae. Flat ceramic disks replaced the compound eyes of a true insect, but Kinsolving saw only the similarities and not the differences.

The robot hunter launched itself with the silence of a true predator on the hunt. Fat blue sparks jumped from its whip-antennae as it gained speed over the rough terrain.

Kinsolving stood still, waiting, waiting, waiting. He had one chance to survive. When the robot came within ten meters he lifted the stun rod and pressed the trigger button. A small hum sounded.

The robot hunter surged forward, unaffected. Kinsolving almost panicked and fled. To have done so would have meant his death. He held his ground and repeatedly triggered the stun rod. One antenna exploding from the ray was Kinsolving's only victory before the robot smashed hard into him, knocking him flat on his back.

He reached up and grabbed at the slippery metal body. No purchase. His hands locked behind the robot's back. With all the strength he had left, Kinsolving applied the bear hug. He yelped when he received a powerful electric shock. He felt flesh searing, his chest muscles jerking with the current. He dared not stop. He again twisted savagely to dislodge the robot. The robot rolled to one side, its repulsor field whining shrilly. As they rolled down the hill, the robot's other antenna snapped off.

This boosted Kinsolving's morale. He applied even more power to his death grip. Rocks tore at his skin, grazed his forehead, cut a portion from one earlobe. He clung to the struggling robot as if his life depended on it—and it did.

Grunting, Kinsolving got his knees under him. With all his strength, he twisted and smashed the robot hunter into a small boulder. The machine's repulsor field died. Through its casing, he felt the fading of its internal power. Kinsolving tossed the dead robot aside and leaned back to rest. He mopped off some of the blood oozing from a half dozen cuts, then realized he had no time for this.

Cameron still prowled the area. His robot might be deactivated but the human hunter remained at large and as deadly as ever.

Kinsolving bent and fumbled at the releases at the side of the robot hunter to get to its internal computer. He failed. On impulse, he pulled out Director Liu's identicard and touched it to the lock. The access panel slid open to reveal the robot's block circuit memory. Kinsolving plucked it free.

If the robot had "memorized" his scent as Cameron had claimed, a new robot would have to be used—and one without the benefit of that sensory imprint. A quick survey of the insides showed that his stun rod had been more effective than he'd thought. Small circuits had overloaded. The robot hunter hadn't been stopped, but it had been impaired enough for Kinsolving to wrestle it to death.

Kinsolving searched for his stun rod but failed to

find it. Rather than waste precious time hunting for it and possibly being found by Cameron, the man started down the path leading from the park.

The city was a trap for him. Nowhere to turn, nowhere to run. But boldness and courage had aided him this far. He had nothing to lose attempting another daring move. Feet pounding hard, he ran from the park. All the way he imagined Cameron's hand descending to his shoulder to stop him, to pull him around and administer the death blow.

It never came.

He returned to Interstellar Materials' headquarters. Liu's identicard still opened doors. With a little luck, he could even find Lark Versalles at the anniversary party.

But what then? Barton Kinsolving had no idea.

CHAPTER TWENTY

BARTON KINSOLVING smoothed off the dirt from his dress clothing and tried to minimize the wrinkles and tears by tucking what he could in under belts and behind a curiously buttoned jacket. The cuts on his face had to be left untended. He doubted anyone would notice—not yet, at least. When Cameron found his pet robot hunter destroyed, the city wouldn't be a fit place to be seen unless every identicard entry matched the one in Interstellar Materials' main computer banks.

Kinsolving fingered Director Liu's identicard and the other card keys he'd stolen. How much longer would these be useful? One careless moment using them and Kinsolving might call down the entire IM security force.

He entered the lobby and skirted the tight knot of people near the center by hugging the wall. It took twice as long to reach the elevators, but caution rather than speed ruled him now. He hoped that Cameron would scour the city for him. Returning to the heart of IM's power—and those who had concocted the Stellar Death Plan—would be suicidal.

Kinsolving hoped that Cameron thought along those lines. It was all that gave the man any chance for escape.

The elevator took him directly to the one-hundred-first floor where the party had become an orgy. Kinsolving's upbringing hadn't been prudish, but such wanton behavior unnerved him. He had no idea how to act, how to react when confronted with licentiousness.

"Barton darling!" came a familiar voice. With relief, Kinsolving turned to see Lark Versalles hurrying toward him, a man and a woman in tow. "I want you to meet two of my dearest friends. This is Dinky and this gorgeous whiff of nebula dust is Rani du-Long. Rani arrived just after we did but she's made up for lost time."

Lark took a long, critical look at Kinsolving. "Whatever have you been doing, darling? You really ought to take your clothes off before doing it, whatever it is."

"I agree," said Rani, moving close to Kinsolving. Her fingers slipped through tears in his shirt and stroked over bare flesh. She curled her fingers slightly and began tugging. The ripping of cloth sounded, even over the raucous music and the boisterous laughter from the party goers. "Such a nice ...friend you have, Lark."

"He's all mine, dear," Lark said, slipping between them.

"What a pity. We've always shared before. Aren't we friends?" Rani's hot gaze made Kinsolving increasingly uneasy. He couldn't tell if her dress had been designed to reveal all that it did or if it had been torn off by some overly amorous suitor.

Seeing the dark-haired woman's response when she saw his own tattered finery, Kinsolving thought she might enjoy ripping clothes before enjoying other pursuits.

"I've got to talk to you, Lark. In private."

"Oh, all right. But just for a moment. Dinky wants this dance, and I did promise." Lark looked over her shoulder, reached out and lightly stroked the man's strong, square chin. Kinsolving noted the laser scalpel scars where cosmetic surgery had been performed to give a weak jawline solidity.

He spun Lark around and said quickly, "We've got to leave. I'm in real trouble."

"Didn't you find anyone to take your case to Chairman Fremont?" Lark frowned. "What a shame. I'll see what I can do. There are several junior vice presidents who owe me a favor. I'm sure one might take up your case. And if not, it will be fun trying."

"No, wait," he said. "There's been a change, a discovery." He licked his lips, not knowing how to phrase this. "I came across some records that people in IM don't want revealed."

"So promise not to divulge them. That's easy." Lark's bright blue eyes stared ingenuously at him. Kinsolving had to wonder if she were really this innocent or if it were a pose. He couldn't tell.

"What I found makes me more valuable dead than alive."

"Over some silly ore thefts?" Lark sniffed elegantly.

"The records have been altered. There's no way I can be accused of the rare earth thefts since it doesn't appear that they ever occurred."

"No one stole the ore?"

"The records have been changed to show that. The theft happened—and I know who is responsible. But Humbolt can't be indicted, and he's done such a good job, neither can I."

"Then there's no problem. What is *wrong*, Barton darling?"

"There's still the charge of murder. The Lorr agent-captain."

"Hmm, yes, that is serious, but they wouldn't turn you over to the aliens. Plead something-or-another. Do your sentence in an Earth prison."

"What would you say if I uncovered a plot by ex-

ecutives in Interstellar Materials to kill entire
planets—entire races!—of aliens?"

"What do you mean?"

"The rare earths are being used to manufacture
electronic devices that other species use as we do
drugs. The difference is that the devices will first
addict, then kill."

"They shouldn't stray from eng-drugs." Lark
reached into a small sash and drew forth a tiny box.
The top popped open and a tiny tube rose. At the
bottom of the golden box Kinsolving saw a light
purple powder, an engineered drug popular with
those able to afford it. "I had this made for my own
brain chemistry, but I'm sure it will do you a world
of good. Try it, Bart."

He looked at the box and recoiled slightly. A
quick sniff would alter his mood in whatever fashion Lark Versalles thought the most enticing. And
it would leave no physical trace, being engineered
for its nonaddictive nature. The electronic devices
IM—or some at the company—proposed would do
far more. Thrills, excitement, habituation, addic-
tion, permanent brain damage, those were the results of their project.

"They mean to kill entire planets of people."

"Of aliens," she said. "They're hardly people.
Well, they *are* but they're not our kind. You know
what I mean."

"We don't have time to argue this. I've found out
about their plan. They don't dare let me live to tell
anyone about it."

"Who're 'they?'" Lark asked.

"I . . ." Kinsolving looked across the dance floor at
the gyrating men and women. Which of these people *were* responsible? He couldn't believe that Humbolt alone conceived their Stellar Death Plan.
A hand lightly brushed over the pocket where he
had placed Director Liu's key cards. Liu had to

be a part of the Plan, too. He had carried the blank access card.

But who else knew, who else in Interstellar Materials planned on a slaughter vaster than anything in Earth history? He saw the joyous faces, the taut faces, the strained, tense faces. Which of these also contorted in fear and hatred to order the deaths of billions of intelligent alien beings?

"We've got to go, Lark. Please, before it's too late." Kinsolving felt the noose tightening around him. Cameron had been careless twice. Expecting him to make the same mistake a third time seemed out of the question.

"I promised this dance to Dinky. Then we'll talk." Lark spun away, laughing and smiling at her friends. He watched her slip into the circle of Dinky's arms and glide away, gracefully moving in time with the music.

Kinsolving shifted nervously from foot to foot, wanting to leave, yet needing Lark. He had to get back into orbit to the *Nightingale*. No other escape opened to him. By the time Cameron finished his cordon, the Gamma Tertius 4 Landing Authority might not allow any vessel to shift from orbit.

"Shall we do it?" came a sultry voice. Kinsolving jumped.

"Shall we do what?" he asked, seeing that Rani duLong had returned.

"Dance," she said, her eyes challenging him. "Unless you can think of something more interesting."

"Later," he said.

"Then we dance." Rani took him in a surprisingly strong grip and whirled him to the center of the dance floor. Kinsolving had never considered himself a good dancer but with the sinuous grace shown by Rani, anyone looked better.

"Lark speaks well of you. She says that you're more exciting than anyone she's met in the past couple years." Rani rubbed seductively against him. "What are your hidden talents?"

"I keep her amused by my, uh, antics," Kinsolving said lamely. He almost stopped the dance and begged off when he saw Cameron enter. Fear surged. He held his rampaging emotions in check and whirled Rani into the center of the crowd.

"You're sweating," Rani said. "Am I that hot?"

"Yes," he said. Kinsolving whirled her around and around until the woman threw back her head and let her long midnight black hair sail forth in a wide circle. She laughed, a sound as pure and clean as ringing silver bells.

"You do have your moments," she said, dark eyes fixed on him. "I'd like to find out more about them —and see if I can't turn them into hours, or even days."

"After the dance," Kinsolving insisted. He kept most of the dancers between him and Cameron. Beside the gaudily dressed man hovered two robot hunters. From the occasional glimpses Kinsolving got, these robot hunters were different from the one he had destroyed in the park. With thicker casings and more heavily armored parts, these might have been war machines reduced in size for use within the city.

Cameron would relish the use of such deadly machines. Kinsolving might have defeated himself by destroying the lesser robot hunter. He had only given Cameron an excuse to use more powerful robots.

"Are you avoiding someone?" Rani asked.

"What if I am?"

"Oh, you men. You're all alike. I'm an expert at avoiding people I don't want to meet again. Or at meeting people I do." She moved slightly out of tempo with the music and slipped across Kinsolving's body so that he moaned softly in response.

"Now. Who is it you want to avoid? I'll show you how."

"The man in the emerald green jacket and pink ruffled shirt."

"Actually," she said, "it's salmon. But I do see him. He has a strange look about him. So cold, in spite of the radiance of his clothing."

"What's he doing?"

"How peculiar. He went directly to Lark. She's leaving with him. She and Dinky. No, Dinky's staying behind. Odd. I've never seen him give up a dance partner so easily."

Kinsolving swung about and got a quick glimpse of Cameron leaving with Lark. The two robot hunters flanked them. The robot nearest Lark emitted tiny blue sparks from one antenna. The first hint of escape would produce a nasty shock—or even death. Kinsolving couldn't discount Cameron's ruthlessness. But why take Lark? Had they somehow connected her with him?

"Cameron is arresting her," he told Rani.

"Lark? Arrested? Oh, this is cosmic! She'll have stories to tell for years to come. What did this Cameron arrest her for? Something you two are responsible for? Oh, yes, yes!" Rani cried. "You're a smuggler. How romantic. What did you smuggle, Barton?"

"You make it sound as if they'll let her go in an hour or so."

"Why not? She hasn't done anything. Not really. Smuggling is hardly enough of a crime to hold Lark Versalles!"

"What if they killed her? What if Cameron took her to the top of this building and shoved her off the roof?"

"But he couldn't. It's airless at the top. Lark wouldn't be able to breathe."

Kinsolving said nothing. The idea slowly penetrated that he meant what he said. Rani's expression changed from confusion to outrage. "He wouldn't dare harm her!"

"I saw him murder a Lorr on Deepdig. Cameron is capable of anything."

"But an alien is, well, an *alien*. We're talking about Lark!"

"A life's a life to Cameron—an alien or human one is equally as cheap."

"We'll see about this. Who's his superior?" Rani's anger rose now. One of her friends had gotten into real trouble. Kinsolving admired her loyalty but not her proposed method.

How could he know which of the IM executives knew of the Plan? All? Some? Which? Glancing around the room he saw none of the highest level. No director or senior vice president was in attendance, even though dozens of the junior executives frolicked and politicked.

"Director Liu," he said, realization coming to him. "That's why Cameron took Lark."

"Lark was with the director earlier," said Rani. "She bragged about it. But why should this Cameron object? Unless he and Director Liu..."

"No, not that," said Kinsolving. He had drawn Lark deeper into this intrigue than he'd intended. Cameron had checked the elevator record to see which identicard had been used. Director Liu had found his card case missing. The conclusion: Lark Versalles had stolen the key cards.

"What should we do?" Rani duLong asked.

"I don't know. I just don't know." Barton Kinsolving tried to hold back a rising tide of helplessness and failed.

CHAPTER TWENTY-ONE

"I'M CERTAIN it's all a misunderstanding. Lark will be able to talk her way out of it. Or maybe," Rani duLong said, leering slightly, "have something of a new adventure getting away from this Cameron. After all, he's only a man."

Kinsolving wouldn't have wagered on that. He had seen the demonic glee in Cameron's eyes when he had killed. The robots accompanying him were also killers. No one commanded such dangerous machines unless their use aided a mission.

Cameron's mission had to be killing. Nothing else fit. The foppish exterior hid a cold, cunning attitude.

"He's a supporter of their Plan," Kinsolving said. "He doesn't dare release Lark, not if he thinks she knows anything about it."

"Plan? What plan?" asked Rani. "Oh, I know."

"What? You do?" asked Kinsolving, his mind light years from all that happened around him.

"I've got the perfect plan. Let Lark suffer for a while, then rescue her. Until then, let's dance." Rani smiled wickedly. "Unless you can think of something else you'd prefer to do—together."

"Rescue," mused Kinsolving. He had to help Lark Versalles. Because she had aided him she now found herself in serious danger. He owed her his life for getting him off the alien prison world, if nothing else. She hadn't asked to be involved.

Rescue. How? No scheme surfaced. He allowed
Rani to lead him to the dance floor. Mechanically
moving his feet, hardly noticing the lovely woman
in his arms, Kinsolving thought. Hard.

The card keys he'd stolen from Director Liu
should be discarded. Their use would trigger
alarms. Cameron would send a robot hunter to the
spot of usage within minutes. Kinsolving didn't
even know where Lark had been taken. To the barren suite of rooms devoted to the Stellar Death
Plan? Possibly, though he doubted it. Most of the
headquarters building was deserted today, the employees at parties or taking a holiday. Interstellar
Materials was nothing if not generous in this re-
spect.

A director's office? Kinsolving doubted that, too,
unless Kenneth Humbolt personally conducted the
woman's interrogation. From all that Kinsolving
had seen of Cameron, the gaudy manhunter
wouldn't want to share the task. He'd consider it a
pleasure, even a thrill in some sexual way.

Kinsolving shuddered. His mind refused to grasp
the fact that these people were capable of any atroc-
ity. Any group able to contemplate the extinction of
entire races wouldn't hesitate at the rape and torture of a single woman if they thought she had information they needed.

"Are you cold, Barton, or just anticipating?" Rani
asked. He stared at the beautiful woman in wonder.
She seemed oblivious to all that he'd said. She
couldn't believe that Lark Versalles was in danger.

"Do you know the headquarters building well?"

"Not really. I've only been here a few times for
parties. Dinky has a small place on the other side of
the city, though. He spends a good part of his time
on GT 4. He does. Why?"

Kinsolving already guided Rani off the dance
floor. He scanned the crowd and found Dinky

propped against a wall, leaning over a chair and trying not to collapse totally. Kinsolving dragged Rani after him. By the time they arrived at Dinky's side, the man had slumped over the chair and snored loudly.

"He's not much help." Rani stared at the man in contempt. "This isn't the only time he falls asleep, either."

Kinsolving sat down beside the unconscious man and shook him hard. Dinky groaned and mumbled something incoherent. Kinsolving steeled himself. He had been raised to avoid harming others. He took Dinky's earlobe and pinched down hard enough to cause a tiny crescent of blood to form. The pain lanced directly into the man's brain past the haze of the drugs he'd taken.

"Whatsit?" he demanded.

"Conference rooms. Where?" demanded Kinsolving.

"Director's rooms?" Dinky said, eyes still not focused.

"What level?"

"One-eighty, one-eighty-one."

Kinsolving sucked in a deep breath and held it for a long minute before slowly releasing it. This building was too immense to search floor by floor. He had to hope that Cameron had taken Lark to one of those levels.

"Do you want to play a new game?" he asked Dinky, talking to the young man as if he were a small child.

"Photonic!" cried Rani. "To hell with him. *I'd* like to play!"

"Great. The two of you can try it." Kinsolving fumbled out the stolen identicard and the card keys. "Here's how you play. Go to the lobby and wait for five minutes. Then try to see how many different places these cards will take you. Elevators, secured areas, everywhere."

"And?" prompted Rani.

"The one who gets into the most places, uh," Kinsolving stumbled here. What would be adequate prize for these jaded sybarites? "The one who gets into the most places wins and the other has to do anything the winner wants for one hour."

"Anything?"

"Anything," Kinsolving agreed solemnly.

Kinsolving fanned through the cards. He had five. He held them up for her to see. "You choose a card. And you, too, Dinky. And find three others to join in."

"You're not playing?" asked Rani, obviously disappointed. Her interest in this "game" extended only to winning Kinsolving for the promised hour. He looked at the card keys, then slipped the blank one into his pocket. It would be very dangerous to allow those besotted revellers to blunder into that special level—it might mean their instant death.

Kinsolving wanted confusion, not death.

"I'll play using the blank card. I'm not sure what it's good for, anyway," he lied.

"Morganna and Chakki will want to play. Come along, Dinky. Let's find them." She turned dark, blazing eyes on Kinsolving. "We start in the lobby in five minutes?"

He nodded, smiling now. Rani thought it was for her. She need not know that Kinsolving had no intention of playing and that there would never be a winner in this mad, dangerous game.

Except Lark, if he could find her.

Kinsolving watched Rani help Dinky to the elevator. Two others followed closely, engaged in animated conversation. The man—Kinsolving had already forgotten his name—seemed reluctant.

Morganna urged him along, and this was enough to get him to play.

They vanished into the elevator and Kinsolving went into action. Dinky had mentioned two possible levels where Lark might be. Kinsolving didn't dare spend the time searching those floors. He entered an empty elevator and ordered it to take him to the one hundred-eightieth floor. Kinsolving held his breath as the doors slid back silently. He expected to see a smiling Cameron waiting for him, both robot hunters hovering at his side.

The corridor stretching to a panorama of crystal windows at the far side of the building loomed silent and ominously deserted. Kinsolving listened for the slightest sound and heard nothing, but he had hardly expected to. All rooms in IM's headquarters were soundproofed. Lark might be screaming in a room only a few paces away and he would never hear.

He dashed to a receptionist's desk and scanned the control console. The complex array of indicators daunted him. It took a trained operator to use it to its fullest. But all Kinsolving needed was a moment's worth of information.

He seated himself and held the blank card key over the identi-slot. A sudden thought hit him. He smiled slowly and put the card back into his pocket and drew out the duplicate of his original identicard given him at the Landing Authority. Cameron hadn't had time to enter a lock on this card—he might not have learned Kinsolving had reactivated his employee card.

Kinsolving paused, then boldly acted. His personal identicard slid into the acceptor.

"How may I serve you, Supervisor Kinsolving?" the computer asked.

"I need to know the location of at least two directors. They must be in the headquarters building and they must be together."

"Three directors are present in room 18117."

Kinsolving wobbled a little in the seat. "Are two of the directors Humbolt and Liu?"

"Yes."

Kinsolving wondered who the third might be. He hesitated to ask for this information, fearing that the computer would alert them.

"Cancel all request."

"Thank you, Supervisor." The screen went dark again. Kinsolving fought down real fear as he reinserted the card and once more was greeted by the computer.

"Monitor restricted elevator usage from level one-eighty-one," he ordered. Kinsolving waited anxiously. Rani and the others ought to be using Liu's stolen cards all over the building by now. That would alert Cameron; Kinsolving hoped the man would personally see to this new problem and go chasing off in four different directions.

A minute. Two. Kinsolving thought he would die of frustration waiting. He jumped when the computer said, "Directors Humbolt and Villalobos, accompanied by one assistant and three robot servants are descending to level thirty-two."

"Cancel," Kinsolving snapped. He grabbed his identicard. It might never be useful again, but he could only hope. Slowness in cancellation thus far had been a boon to him. It might continue.

He took the elevator to the floor above. If Humbolt and the others had taken the director's private elevator, he need not fear discovery; that elevator lay on the far side of the building. Kinsolving entered the deserted corridor, a duplicate of the floor below. Slowly, carefully, he looked around each corner as he made his way to 18117. In front of the door, he paused.

Lark wouldn't be unguarded. Kinsolving guessed that the "human assistant" with Humbolt and Villalobos was Cameron. If that supposition proved wrong, he would be in serious trouble.

If he didn't act quickly, he would be in even more serious danger—and Lark's life would be forfeit.

Kinsolving touched the door frame and the panel slid open silently. Lark was held against a far wall by a single band circling her waist and fastened into the wall. Her blue eyes widened when she saw him, but Kinsolving didn't have to warn her to silence. She realized her only hope of rescue lay with him.

"But, Director," she said too loudly, "why are you doing this? I don't know anything. My daddy is going to be *extremely* upset with you. With Interstellar Materials!"

"I'm sorry for this, my dear," Liu said. "But even your father won't be able to solve your problem. Where is your companion? Where is Kinsolving?"

Kinsolving didn't give the man a fair chance. He folded his hands together in a double fist and swung as hard as he could. The impact on the back of Liu's head sent the director forward onto his face. He groaned once, jerked, then lay still.

"Did you kill him?" asked Lark.

"Don't think so. How do you open this?" Kinsolving searched for the release. Only a card acceptor looked promising.

"That. They used a card. The one with Director Humbolt. Cameron."

The steel band tightly held her to the wall. Noting less than a cutting torch would free Lark—or Cameron's card key.

"Here goes nothing," Kinsolving said, pulling out the blank card key. He inserted it. A soft click sounded and Lark Versalles tumbled free.

"Thank you, Barton darling. I *knew* you'd come.

This has been ever so much fun. But Director Liu *did* make me mad. How dare he chain me like this!"

"Come on," Kinsolving said. He had a bad feeling about using the special card key. The use of the stolen cards had triggered alarms to alert Cameron. This one would, also. This card of all those taken would be most likely to draw attention.

"Where are we going?"

"To the directors' private elevator," he said. Something alerted Kinsolving just before they turned the corner to the elevator. He shoved Lark into an office and clamped a hand over her mouth. She struggled for a moment, then settled down, her arms around him and her head on his shoulder. He left a finger between door and jamb, giving a restricted field of view into the hallway.

Cameron and a robot hunter glided by silently. Kinsolving counted to ten, then slid two more fingers into the slit and tugged the door open. Cameron had just turned the corner. Kinsolving motioned for Lark to hurry. They went to the directors' elevator. Again Kinsolving dared to use the blank card key—for the last time. Any more usage carried too great a risk.

The door slid open and the pleasant voice asked, "Floor?"

"Lobby," he said.

"Thank you, sir."

The elevator sank swiftly to the lobby. He feared the worst when the door opened, but no platoon of security guards descended like vultures on carrion. If anything, the lobby seemed more deserted now than it had been earlier.

"This is *so* exciting," Lark cooed. "Picking you off that silly alien world has been such an adventure." Lark kissed Kinsolving soundly.

"No time for that. We've got to get away, get off Gamma Tertius 4. Cameron and the others will be looking for us. And this time they won't be so gentle if they catch you."

"I'm really very vexed with them," Lark said. "Director Liu acted so rudely. And I must say that the dark woman—the one pretty in a dark sort of way, if you like the type—insulted me. Imagine!"

"Villalobos?" he asked. Kinsolving had seen the director only at the opening ceremony.

"Yes, she's the one."

"They've locked the lobby doors," he said suddenly. "There's no other reason not to have guards patrolling everywhere."

His fears proved accurate. "Sorry, sir, access is denied," said the mechanical voice. "Only Class four and higher passed allowed."

"I'm a Class five," he said. "Supervisor level." Kinsolving put his identicard into the acceptor slot. He thought a thunderbolt had sounded; the door lock had opened.

"Come on," he said, dragging Lark behind him. He retrieved his identicard but knew it would be of no use to him again. Cameron still hadn't learned of the duplicate card being issued by the LA. But he would. Each of the stolen card keys would be tracked down now, no matter how much Rani and the others dodged and ran, trying to win the "game" Kinsolving had set up for them.

"Where are we going?" asked Lark.

Barton Kinsolving stopped and stared up into the starlit dome of atmosphere over the city.

"I don't know," he said.

All escape seemed cut off now. He had done well to this point, but luck had run out.

CHAPTER TWENTY-TWO

"IT'S COLD," complained Lark Versalles. "The wind is killing me." She pulled the skirt of the blue dress up and tried to hide behind it like a little girl might. Kinsolving had no sympathy for her. She was worried about trivial matters; he sought a way for them to survive.

"There's a small rocky alcove I know in a park," he said. Kinsolving cursed his lack of knowledge of Interstellar Materials' corporate city. He had been lucky to stay alive by doubling back, returning to the spots where Cameron wouldn't think to look. Did he try that tactic once too often? Would Cameron find Director Liu unconscious and Lark freed and immediately guess that Kinsolving returned to the park?

Kinsolving had no way of knowing what a true predator would think. But he would have to learn or die.

He shielded Lark from the wind as much as he could as they followed the hard-packed trail into the cul-de-sac. The view of the city surprised him. The lights shone clear, pure and distinct. No pollution marred an exquisite view. He wished that he and Lark had come to this spot under different circumstances.

"This is better," she said. "But it's even nicer when you put your arm around me." She burrowed close, her face almost hidden in the front of his battered coat.

"We need to get off GT 4," he told her. "We can't use the shuttle service. Cameron will have guards waiting for us."

"Director Liu accused me of stealing his card keys. You took them, didn't you?"

He admitted that he had. "I used them for access to a special floor." His eyes turned to the immense glass spire rising in the center of the city. "What I found there is why they want to kill me—us."

"Do you want to tell me? I deserve to know."

Kinsolving considered. Telling Lark did nothing to further jeopardize her. If Cameron or his robot hunters caught her now, they would kill her. The more who know of the Stellar Death Plan, the better the chance of stopping it.

"Someone—maybe all the directors—has worked out a plan to destroy entire alien populations."

"Why?"

Kinsolving shook his head. This went against the teachings of every instructor in college. Earth had adopted a policy of accepting its second-rate place in galactic society—temporarily. By work and application and learning to live with the scores of other, alien intelligent races Earth might rise and take its place as an equal.

That was what he'd been taught. That was what Barton Kinsolving believed.

"I've heard Humbolt say that the aliens are intentionally holding Earth back, keeping us a minor power."

"It seems that way at times," Lark said. "But there are so many of them and so few of us, why should they?"

"Exactly. We're a nuisance, but not a threat. We're the brash newcomer who has to find a spot to fit in.

I don't think any of the aliens seek to destroy us. They hardly even know we exist."

"What's the plan to get rid of them?"

"It's ruthless and dangerous," said Kinsolving, going cold inside. He hugged Lark tighter without realizing that he did so. "Humbolt has been pirating rare earths from the mines on Deepdig. After he fixed the records to show smaller liftings, the rare earths are sent to an assembly plant. I don't know where." Kinsolving heaved a sigh. "I thought at first their plan was just to rob the Lorr of taxes. It's more. The plants use cerium to build electronic devices that act like drugs do on humans."

"You don't mean these will help the aliens enjoy themselves?" asked Lark. She frowned. Kinsolving took that as a good sign. The woman understood.

"The devices are illegal. Humbolt and the others smuggle them in to planets like Zeta Orgo 4, the natives use them and become helplessly addicted. Eventually the device burns out their brains. I got the hint that it might even induce others near the unit to use it more until they, too, died, their brains turned to charcoal."

"This doesn't sound illegal as much as it does immoral," said Lark.

"The devices are engineered to addict and destroy. Imagine allowing the sale of drugs that only killed."

"This still doesn't seem *that* bad," said Lark. "The aliens don't have to use *any* gadget, much less the ones furnished by Humbolt."

"I think they do. The evidence I saw in the files is sketchy but the simple operation of the machine is addictive. Anyone within a few meters needs more stimulation. And then more and more until the brain is physically short-circuited."

"What would the aliens do if they found out about this?"

"I don't know. Among their own people, they

might send them off to that prison world." Kinsolving spoke without a quaver in his voice. "If they think there is a concerted effort by the part of IM employees—or Interstellar Materials itself—the consequences might be dire. They might decide to destroy Gamma Tertius 4."

"The entire planet?"

"Most of the alien races have that power." Kinsolving swallowed hard. "They might decide that Earth is the cause and destroy it."

"Maybe it's better if we don't tell anyone," suggested Lark. "If the aliens find out ..."

"Is it better to let Humbolt and the others destroy billions of intelligent people for the sake of their xenophobia?"

"No," she answered. "How can we stop them? I mean, I'm no crusader. I don't want to do this, but it's so ... wrong."

"We've got to get off GT 4," Kinsolving said. "How, I can't say. It wouldn't do to steal a shuttle, even if we could. I'm sure that there are defensive weapons in orbit around the planet. If Humbolt is crazy enough to think all the aliens want to destroy mankind, he's crazy enough to defend against a threat that doesn't exist."

Kinsolving held Lark even tighter as a blast of cold wind gusted around a rocky precipice. What would they do, even if they succeeded in getting to orbit? Locking the *Nightingale* would be too simple to do. Cameron might have overlooked deactivating Kinsolving's identicard and flagging it in the company computer, but that had been a small oversight. Cameron wouldn't make many more—if any.

"We can stow away," Lark said. "Oh, this might be fun! You see it all the time in the tri-vid dramas. We stow away, get into orbit and then find a starship to stow away in."

The woman made it sound so simple.

"Launch mass is carefully measured," he told her. "We might be able to get to orbit but the *Nightingale* will be... watched."

"You mean locked and off limits." Lark sighed. "I love that ship. We've done so much together. But I imagine Daddy can get it back. All he has to do is ask."

"You make that sound easy."

"I've gone off with friends before and left the *Nightingale.* Then Daddy sends someone to ferry it to another planet. We always manage to make connections." Lark giggled like a small girl. "We can do it that way. Let Daddy worry about the *Nightingale.*"

"What do we do once we get into orbit? I've got an idea on that score, but—"

"Oh, that's not hard. We just wait for Rani. She'd give us a free ride anywhere we want. She owes me. Besides," Lark said in a harsher tone, "she obviously wants you. That's all my fault, I suppose. I shouldn't have told her how much fun you are."

"Rani," he said. Kinsolving's mind raced. The dark-haired woman and her friends would be in custody by now. "Is she someone important?"

"Rani duLong? I should say so. Her brother is chief executive officer of TerraComp."

Kinsolving shook his head. TerraComp wasn't the largest Earth-based computer manufacturer but its market gave it incredible potential. He couldn't see Humbolt risking the life of the sister of TerraComp's CEO.

Besides, what had Rani done? She used a few card keys to run around IM headquarters, nothing more. It had all been a part of the anniversary party fun and games. Cameron wouldn't kill Rani or Dinky or the other two—he would just escort them off-planet.

Immediately.

"We've got to get to the Landing Authority, right now!" Kinsolving exclaimed. "I used Rani to create a diversion while I freed you. Humbolt and Villalobos will deport Rani without hesitation, anniversary party be damned. When they do, we've got to be ready."

"For what?" asked Lark.

Kinsolving had no answer. But when the opportunity presented itself, they had to be alert enough to take it.

"I can't walk another micron, Bart. I don't know why you're torturing me like this."

"There wasn't any way we could use public transportation without being noticed," he explained again to the complaining woman. "My identicard is flagged by now. And so is yours."

"Nonsense. My credit's good. Always has been. Oh, you mean Cameron would use it to trace us. I don't see why that's so bad. He knows we're heading for the LA."

Kinsolving had to admit Lark had a point. Simply hiding in the city gained him nothing. They had to leave Gamma Tertius 4 or be caught eventually. All Cameron needed to do was cordon off the Landing Authority and wait. Sooner or later they would blunder into the guards and be taken.

Kinsolving smiled wickedly. Catching them wouldn't be *that* easy. He had learned much.

He sobered. Too much rested on his escape. Humbolt had to be stopped before the mind-burn device was sent to alien worlds like Zeta Orgo 4. Discovery by the aliens might mean the destruction of Earth, but Kinsolving didn't want entire populations of alien planets to be destroyed, either. How he could walk this tightwire he didn't know.

But he had to try.

"The LA isn't fenced," he said. "There's no need

because everyone coming here is on company business."

"GT's hardly the garden and vacation spot of the universe," Lark said dryly.

Kinsolving watched as robotic sniffers worked on every vehicle entering the main entrance. At points surrounding the launch site robot hunters patrolled. He saw occasional metallic glints off heavy body casing and whiplike antennae. Getting past them would be impossible.

Getting past the sniffers would merely be difficult.

"Barton, look. Isn't that Cameron?"

Lark pointed to a vehicle waiting in the line for admittance to the LA. The vehicle immediately behind had four people huddled into the rear. Kinsolving recognized Dinky's head and assumed the other three were Rani, Morganna and Chakki.

He jerked hard on her hand and they walked briskly along the path paralleling the roadway. Kinsolving maneuvered around so that Cameron would have to crane about in his seat to see all that happened in the vehicle behind. Stooping, he picked up a large rock and handed it to Lark. She started to ask what he was doing. He gestured for silence, them came up beside the driver and tapped on the window.

"What is it?" demanded the driver.

"Those Mr. Cameron's prisoners?" Kinsolving asked.

"Who're you?"

"Landing Authority clearance," Kinsolving said, "Open the door, will you?"

"You don't look like an official," the man said, opening his door. "Let me check with Cameron."

He never got any farther. Lark hit him with the rock Kinsolving had given her. Kinsolving pushed the man back into the vehicle and stripped off his jacket. Time crushed down heavily on him. His fingers felt as if they had turned into stubby sausage. He was sure that Cameron would turn around and see what happened behind. Already the line of vehicles began to move.

"There," he said triumphantly, getting the jacket off the guard. Kinsolving slipped into it, wincing as seams split on the too-small garment. He grabbed the front of the man's shirt and heaved, tossing him out and onto the path alongside the roadway. In a few minutes, he would either recover or be noticed.

By then Kinsolving hoped to be in space.

"What's going on?" came Rani's curious voice. "Why, it's you, Barton. And Lark! Oh, this is ever so exciting. You didn't lie when you said it was all—"

"Quiet!" Kinsolving snapped. "Keep quiet until we're in orbit."

"They're taking us to our ships," said Rani. "Are you two going to stow away on the *von Neumann?*" Kinsolving nodded. "Photonic! Lark, dear, we're going to be the envy of everyone when we tell them about this. Escape from brutal guards on Gamma Tertius 4!"

Kinsolving edged the vehicle forward, keeping his head down when Cameron turned and pointed at them. Cameron gunned his vehicle and shot forward, toward a shuttle readying for launch. Kinsolving pulled even with the guards. The robotic sniffers emitted shrill warnings.

"Wait," the guard said as Kinsolving started to accelerate through. "The alarms went off."

"Of course they did, idiot," snapped Kinsolving. "Mr. Cameron told you that these people were being shipped out, didn't he? Deported?"

"Yes, but—"

"They're all in the computer as undesirables. You should worry if there *wasn't* an alarm sounded."

"He said there were four. I count five back there."

"You misunderstood him. Look, Mr. Cameron's a very impatient man, if you know what I mean. You call him back to verify something this minor, you take the blame."

The guard looked across the tarmac toward the shuttle. Cameron had already started to pace. He presented the perfect picture of a man ready to explode in anger. The guard motioned Kinsolving through without another word.

"Simply photonic!" cried Rani duLong. "Lark, this is wonderful. Wait until Tia and Pierre hear about our adventure!"

"What are you going to do now?" asked Lark, more concerned than her friend about Cameron.

"Keep in motion. No matter what, keep moving. You and the others get out and then run. Get into the shuttle. I'll be along in a hurry. When I do, we've got to launch. See if you can convince the pilot about that."

"Sounds like an interesting challenge," said Lark.

Kinsolving drove at high speed, then killed the repulsor field suddenly. The vehicle hit the pavement, slewed and sent up a curtain of sparks. Cameron bellowed in anger as he sprinted to get out of the careening car's path. Kinsolving's vehicle crashed into Cameron's and came to a noisy stop. Kinsolving gestured wildly, urging the others to speed. Lark followed instructions and herded them out and up the gangway into the shuttle.

Barton Kinsolving wondered what he ought to do now. In hand-to-hand combat he was no match for Cameron. Although the man didn't seem to have a robot hunter with him, he might be armed. Kinsolving couldn't stand against that.

Kinsolving cast a worried glance up and saw Lark waving from the shuttle air lock. Cameron had drawn the bulky tube from inside his jacket and stalked toward the downed repulsor vehicle.

Kinsolving waited, estimated, waited until he thought his heart would explode, then savagely twisted the repulsor field starter switch. The engine circuits overloaded and shut down almost instantly, but not before the vehicle lifted toward Cameron.

The front of the vehicle struck the man a glancing blow. Cameron screamed and triggered the weapon he held. The aluminum side of the car vanished in a flare of heat and a rain of molten droplets. Kinsolving abandoned the vehicle and scurried up the shuttle gangway, sometimes on hands and knees.

Lark dragged him into the air lock. Kinsolving spun around and sat down heavily. The last sight he had of the GT Landing Authority was Cameron lying facedown on the tarmac, his energy weapon a meter from his outflung hand.

"We did it!" cried Lark.

Kinsolving nodded numbly. The shuttle jerked as the heavy laser buried under the surface began pulsing, lifting them ever higher with every new lightning bolt of energy. They would be in orbit quickly.

What then? They hadn't yet escaped from Cameron. Kinsolving wouldn't believe it until they shifted into hyperspace.

CHAPTER TWENTY-THREE

"THEY'LL STOP US," said Barton Kinsolving. "I know they will. Cameron's not dead. Humbolt beamed out the message." He wrung his hands and sent himself tumbling head over heels in the zero gravity. The shuttle had launched and found its orbit, but Kinsolving worried over the turmoil on the planet below.

"We might not have much time," agreed Lark Versalles, "but we have enough to get to the *Nightingale*."

"No!"

"Why not?" she said petulantly. "I don't want to simply leave it here. I've done that too many times. Daddy is going to get mad."

Kinsolving's mind raced. "The orbiting defense system," he said. "We've got to get away from GT as quickly as possible. I'm sure that Cameron alerted the defense guards to laser the *Nightingale* if we try to get in."

"You're welcome to come with me," came a sultry voice. Kinsolving caught a stanchion and held himself in position to see Rani duLong floating in a hatchway. Her billowing skirt floated seductively around her thighs—an effect she worked hard to achieve.

"Am I invited, too?" Lark asked caustically.

"Of course you are, dear. It might be even more fun if the three of us are together."

"Perhaps not," sniffed Lark.

"Your ship."

"The *von Neumann*," said Rani.

"Is it nearby? Will we be able to board soon?"

"First on this taxi's route," she assured Kinsolving. "We can shift out of the system within, oh, a few hours."

"It takes that long for you to power up?" he asked, astounded. Lark's starship had been fully automated and virtually ran itself.

"Not really. That's the time I'm supposed to take to be sure everything is operational. My brother got mad at me once when I tried taking off too quickly. I did something to the engine. I don't know what. That's hardly my field."

"There's a safety override?" pressed Kinsolving.

"I suppose. I'm sure that you can figure out how to turn it off. You're so...capable." Rani rotated slowly, her skirt flaring around her body as she moved.

"Let's get to your starship as quickly as possible," said Kinsolving. The pressure of time sent his pulse racing. Every instant he thought might be their last. Cameron wouldn't take their escape easily. Turning this shuttle and everyone aboard into superheated plasma might not be company policy, but Kinsolving doubted if many of the directors of Interstellar Materials would complain.

Certainly Kenneth Humbolt, Villalobos and Liu would say nothing. And how many of the others were privy to the diabolical Plan?

"Docking in five," came the pilot's voice over the intercom. "Prepare for docking in five minutes."

"I'll need all my cases," said Rani. A frown marred her perfect features. "That silly Mr. Cameron didn't load them. I don't remember it. Oh, damn!"

"Don't worry," Lark said sweetly. "All your clothing is so out of style that it's better off left behind."

"What about Dinky and the other two?" cut in Kinsolving. "Are they going to be all right?"

"The shuttle will take them to their ships. Imagine being thrown off a planet like Gamma Tertius 4," said Rani. "The indignity." She smiled widely. "The utter *thrill* of it!"

Kinsolving saw that Rani, like Lark, spent her time seeking new sensations, new diversions. He had worked hard all his life. Simply having a job when so many on Earth didn't had been fulfilling for him. Lark and Rani were rich beyond his wildest, most avaricious dreams. For a moment he wondered how he would enjoy such immense wealth, money that allowed him to do as he pleased, roam where he would, see the galaxy firsthand.

Kinsolving found that his imagination didn't extend this far. All he could think of was getting free of Gamma Tertius 4 and trying to warn others of the genocides planned by those working for IM.

And Ala Markken. What of Ala? Her part in the Plan seemed innocuous. Or could anyone taking part in such mass slaughter be innocent? What had become of her after she left Deepdig?

Kinsolving held in his emotions when he realized that a spark still burned for the woman, in spite of what she had done on Deepdig, in spite of her part in sending him to the alien prison world.

"Docking...now!" came the pilot's command. A tremor passed through the shuttle as the hulls came into contact. A deep humming filled the shuttle passenger area; the magnetic grapples held their air lock to that of the starship.

"Do you think I should say good-bye to the others?" asked Lark.

The worry on Kinsolving's face made her abandon such a notion. "I'll see them soon enough. There's always an interesting party or festival where we can talk later."

Kinsolving had barely started the *von Neumann's* air lock cycling shut when the shuttle cut free. The pilot wanted nothing more to do with them. He might not know exactly what had happened at the Landing Authority but it had to mean trouble—and Kinsolving wondered briefly what encouragement Lark had offered the pilot for such a swift and unquestioned flight.

"Can you do something with all this?" asked Rani. She ran her fingers through Kinsolving's hair as he settled into the acceleration couch. Kinsolving looked up when he felt more fingers threading their way across his head. Lark hung suspended on the other side.

"This toggle is the safety override," he said. With a quick movement of the wrist, he freed the ship of the need for a lengthy countdown. His hands worked over the control console until Kinsolving felt as if he played some giant musical instrument.

"We're almost there. We're not supposed to go directly into a shift from such a low orbit, but this is an emergency. We—"

Kinsolving squinted. The forward vidscreen flared twice. Tiny yellow and blue dots danced in front of his eyes.

"What happened? The safety switch? You broke my ship!" complained Rani.

"That was in space," said Lark. Realization dawned on her. She settled down into a couch, hand over her mouth.

"What's wrong?" asked Rani.

"The shuttle," Kinsolving said grimly. "They lasered it. The first flare was the hull vaporizing. The second was the steering rocket fuel exploding."

"But Dinky and ..." Rani fell silent when she understood that those on the planet below had ordered the shuttle and all aboard murdered.

"Time to leave." Kinsolving didn't check to see if Rani and Lark were secured. He toggled the stardrive. The compact ship shifted into hyperspace.

Through the vidscreen Barton Kinsolving got one last look at Gamma Tertius 4. He was leaving behind those who would make themselves masters of all space by brutal murder. They could not be allowed to succeed.

They would not!

"Ala," he said softly, then gave himself over to the senses-twisting effect of the stardrive.

BIO OF A SPACE TYRANT
Piers Anthony

"Brilliant...a thoroughly original thinker and storyteller with a unique ability to posit really *alien* alien life, humanize it, and make it come out alive on the page." *The Los Angeles Times*

A COLOSSAL NEW FIVE VOLUME SPACE THRILLER—
BIO OF A SPACE TYRANT
The Epic Adventures and Galactic Conquests of Hope Hubris

VOLUME I: REFUGEE   84194-0/$3.50 US/$4.50 Can
Hubris and his family embark upon an ill-fated voyage through space, searching for sanctuary, after pirates blast them from their home on Callisto.

VOLUME II: MERCENARY   87221-8/$3.50 US/$4.50 Can
Hubris joins the Navy of Jupiter and commands a squadron loyal to the death and sworn to war against the pirate warlords of the Jupiter Ecliptic.

VOLUME III: POLITICIAN   89685-0/$3.50 US/$4.50 Can
Fueled by his own fury, Hubris rose to triumph obliterating his enemies and blazing a path of glory across the face of Jupiter. Military legend...people's champion...promising political candidate...he now awoke to find himself the prisoner of a nightmare that knew no past.

THE BEST-SELLING EPIC CONTINUES—
VOLUME IV: EXECUTIVE
89834-9/$3.50 US/$4.50 Can
Destined to become the most hated and feared man of an era, Hope would assume an alternate identify to fulfill his dreams ...and plunge headlong into madness.

VOLUME V: STATESMAN
89835-7/$3.50 US/$4.95 Can
the climactic conclusion of Hubris' epic adventures: